DON'T WORRY

DON'T WORRY

SAJID BOLIA

authorHOUSE®

AuthorHouse™
1663 Liberty Drive
Bloomington, IN 47403
www.authorhouse.com
Phone: 1-800-839-8640

Published by AuthorHouse   02/28/2012

ISBN: 978-1-4678-9020-5 (sc)
ISBN: 978-1-4678-9021-2 (e)

INTRODUCTION

In England, a boy by the name of Shakiel does what he needs to survive, whether it pleases him or not. He soon gets himself into situations where society looks down on him, and he has no chance of getting anywhere in life. To make things more complex, he falls for a girl who is spoken for. Shakiel has to somehow get himself out of trouble and get what he wants, but the only thing that can help him is faith.

ABOUT THE AUTHOR

Sajid Bolia is a twenty-five-year-old British-born Asian-African. He graduated with a degree in electronic engineering. Sajid has a passion in writing poems, music, and stories.

Don't Worry is set in England. It tells a story of how having faith can make your dreams come true.

don't worry

By A. Sajid Bolia

Sajid Bolia

ACKNOWLEDGEMENTS

Peace be upon everyone. First of all, this goes out to my mum. For every little thing you've done for me, I appreciate it. Secondly, to my late pops for just being the best. I miss you, Dad. Next, my late *mama*. I miss you so much too. Then to my brothers Mux and Tim for being *tight,* and to my sisters Sara Bai and Shabz for just giving and giving. Thank you. My safe and lovely cousins, aunties, and uncles. Big up to all my mates and people I know from all over: KH, uni, B Town, UK, Africa, worldwide—got too many to name. You know who you are. Maybe in my next book, I might say everyone's names, LOL.

I thank the Almighty the most, for giving me strength and motivation to finish it. Jazakallah. In the time I wrote this book, I finished school, went to college, went to uni, got engaged, and also got married, so I have to give a special shout-out to my beautiful wife, Shamaa. You will always be the greatest blessing given to me. I love you. Anyway, if I forgot to mention you, I big you up the most. Respect.

Oh, yeah . . . The book is written in my lingo. I tried writing it with proper grammar, but thought 'allow it, cousin,' so there's probably bare mistakes.

Illustrations by Abdul-Haqq Sajid Bolia.

CHAPTER 1

It was a warm summer's day. The traffic was slow, windows were rolled down, and people in their T-shirts were loving the weather. Asr had just finished at the *masjid,* and I waited outside for my mates whilst tying my annoying shoelaces. As I knelt down, my wallet slipped out my jacket pocket and opened. Two passport photos, a smaller picture on a piece of paper, and a fiver had fallen out from the wallet. The passport photos were of me, but the small cut-out was of someone I've liked for many years now. I looked up to see if any one saw the picture, but luckily I was in the clear. This person gave me strange butterfly feelings in my stomach every time I spoke to her or even thought of her. She is the reason I go on in life rather than slack back like the other guys, and the worst thing is she doesn't even know a thing about it. I think of her a lot because she's different from other girls.

'Easy bro, you missing to your yard, Shak,' my mate said while slipping his shoes on.

'Yeah, is Asif and them coming?' I replied as I put my wallet in my jeans back pocket.

'Na, Asif and Mo are sitting in for the *deen* talk,' he responded while walking out of the masjid and onto the sidewalk area with me. Quite a few other men were coming out of the masjid, and after a few minutes there was a crowd of Muslim brothers chatting away outside the masjid.

'Let's miss, bro. I think the talk's gonna go on for ages,' I said impatiently.

We walked down the road towards High Street. 'You know about the CD I was meant to give ya. I managed to fit all them tracks you wanted. I was burning it, then my computer crashed and that messed the burning program so ma sister's gonna install it again,' I explained as we reached High Street.

'Don't worry, my grandmother still don't know you making that classics CD for her, but try and do it for tomorrow bro, yeah,' he replied as I nodded.

'Since ma mum passed away, I've got bare close to her and getting to know her past a bit better. It's hard not having a parent, innit bro? Especially your mum. Paradise lies under her feet, so where's paradise for me, bro? I got no mum like,' he sighed while looking directly into my eyes.

I saw that his eyes were slowly starting to water. Boys don't usually look into another boy's eyes, so I knew he was talking deeply. 'Don't worry, bro, you a strong guy, man. My man's givin it to you rough but it's all in his will. When ma pops passed away, I never thought I could live normal any more, but look, I'm cool. I'm still living. You strong, man. Don't worry, inshallah, you'll see her again. Do you still go see her at the *kabarstaan?* You should you know, they know when you visit like,' I advised as he sniffed and pulled out a cigarette.

'True, bro. You got a lighter?' He wiped his nose with his index finger.

'Should do,' I replied as I searched for the lighter. I noticed a bus stopping at the bus stop and a ball going on the road. I passed him the lighter, and he lit his cigarette up, covering his hands to block the wind.

'I go graveyard once in a while, but I get too upset when I'm there. Listen bro, only thing making me live on these days is ma pop, ma grandmother, and ma dope. If I ever lost either one of them, I dunno what I'd do man. Anyways, safe man. Later then, Shak.'

He inhaled his cigarette and turned to cross the road. I took no observations of the traffic, but the oncoming bus dodged a few children while they were getting their ball and *smack!*

"Nooo!"

I was sprayed with blood and pushed back by the force of the impact. The bus's brakes screamed as the body was thrown farther up the road.

I ran to my mate's aid, my heart rapidly pounding. There were screams from the public.

'Help!' I shouted as I saw my mate's forehead cut open. His arms were twisted at the back of him and he was coughing out a lot of blood. I looked at the bus driver through the bloody windscreen; he was in shock and seemed to not know what to do.

'Shak, is that you?' My mate struggled to look as blood poured out of his forehead and onto his eyes.

'Don't worry, Ansar, fight it, bro,' I cried as large amounts of tears fell onto his jacket.

'Shak, it hurts, man, choon the boys I fought for my life. Yeah, looks like I'm gonna see ma mum after all.' He coughed out blood for the last time.

I'm eighteen-year-old Shakiel, and that was twenty-year-old, Ansar, my close friend. He was like an older brother to me, and now he's gone for good. Damn, man!

The funeral. Two days after the death, it was a mild midsummer's afternoon after Asr. I found it really difficult to explain what had happened to Ansar to his other family members, as he kept himself really close to them. I had contacted his father and broken the news on the day of the incident, which was not easy. For two days, the incident has just been repeating itself in my mind, over and over. I explained the story quite a few times to different members of his family today until, 'Yeah, man, he got licked by the bus. I say he be chillin wiv ma nigga Easy, Biggie, Pac . . .' I put it into plain words to his black friend, Marlon.

'Wot d'you say?' Marlon said in disgust.

'I'm sorry, blood. I won't say the N Bomb in front of you again,' I apologised.

'You best not, nigga, or I'm gonna call ma niggaz from the ghetto to bust a cap in yo ass.' Marlon threatened me as he put his clenched fist up.

'Don't worry, I won't say it again,' I responded with my arms covering my face.

As the burial took place, his father led the way in front of his other relatives. They carried the casket to the grave and slowly lowered the casket down. I could see they were really struggling, but I could not help because I could not take in that such a young person was getting buried.

Tears eventually came out of Ansar's father; he was being strong for the past two days but showed he could not keep it in any longer. A few of his relations comforted him and led him back into his car. Tears started coming from other men. My own tears came as well.

'Everyone's gonna miss one day, bro.' I looked up and it was my friend Rizwan from the masjid who came to sit on the bench where I was sitting. He put his arm around me in comfort then smiled. 'Shak, ma mum thinks I'm at college. Do you mind dropping me off because I came with . . .'

'Yeah, I will, don't worry, bro,' I replied. I stood up and took in some fresh air.

'Riz, me and you can *go* any time, you know. I mean, Ansar was only twenty. He was still in depression 'cuz of his mum . . . I feel bare sorry for his pops, man. Did you see how he broke out there?' I whimpered out as I jumped into my car with Rizwan.

'I know, livin wiv two tragedies,' Rizwan said while fastening his seatbelt. I dropped Rizwan at college and then drove straight home.

My mum was cooking and my sister was installing the CD-burning program on my computer.

'I've installed it and made your CD. Why do you want these old tracks anyways? They songs that even Mum would think are *old*. You and your phases, man,' my sister, Tara, confusingly said as she passed me the CD.

'It was for ma mate's grandma, ma mate who passed away, safe for doing it,' I replied whilst taking the CD out of her hands. I looked at it as if it was Ansar's and I was too late to give it to him. I knew if she got it from him, it'd make him more happy to see his grandmother happy.

A week later, at my cousin Majid's house, the moonlight shone directly into his bedroom. I could tell someone was watching me through the gap of the door; I quickly glimpsed and saw a dark figure slowly moving away.

'Bro, you wanna spliff, G?' Majid offered me a roll up.

I rejected as he looked at me funny.

'Wah go at it, bro. You shot someone or something?'

'Nah man, ma mate passed away last week. Got hit by a double-decker,' I answered.

'Ohh, Shibby.' Majid opened the window and lit his spliff up. 'Me and Adil heard 'bout that one. I thought my man got hit wiv a car or something. Anyway, listen, 'cuz things like this happen for reasons, you get me? Remember how ma bro got hit by that muppet taxi driver?'

I nodded.

'Anyways, Shak, you never gave me your keys for a spin at the wedding. Wah go at it wiv that, man?' Majid questioned me.

'Ar soz, man, you know wot it *was*. Your mum was chatting to me about marrying your sister . . . I don't really know your sis that well, so I go na. I'm not blazing, but your sis keeps on givin me evils, you get me?' I tried making a quick comeback as I didn't want him to drive the rental I got out for that day. I knew how reckless he drove.

'Cuz that's what all arranged marriages are all about, not knowing a thing about each other, my time's coming soon. Gonna get married to Dilshad. D's dad wants it as soon as possible, so I go next year, inshallah. Anyways, who you gonna marry then?' asked Majid while bouncing on his bed, lying down.

'Don't tell no one, yeah, but I had a dream, just after ma pops passed away. It was of him, right, at the old yard, you know at Brookside. He goes to me, "Go call Naila from upstairs." So I'm like, "Okay, but wait there, how come you're here, dad, and what's Naila doing here?" He then said that she has to get me ready for something and go. I asked, "Why does *she* need to get me ready?" Then ma dad said it, he said, "She's your wife, isn't she?"' I narrated my dream to Majid.

'But Naila's set up with Ali, you know that, don't you?' Majid clarified.

'Yeah, I know, man. Thing is, since that dream I haven't thought of anyone else. I wanna only marry her,' I said while smiling.

Majid shook his head laughing. 'You're one crazy cousin, Shak. I'd rate ya but that's going into some next situations.'

By any chance, if you were wondering who the picture cut-out was of in my wallet, it's only a picture of my dream girl, Naila.

CHAPTER 2

NOT MUCH HAPPENED in the next year. I failed my A levels; as usual, I have never passed anything before, not even my driving test. I took my driving test three times and failed each time seriously, so I emailed my cousins from back home to forge me my own driving licence. So for about a year and a half I have been driving illegally and never been caught, thankfully.

I really want to pass something one day. I feel I let my mother down too much and I am not a very good big brother for Tara. She thinks I'm hopeless, but I'm not as clever as they think I am. The worst thing is my sister is paying for bills in the house, now that she's seventeen and got a job. I don't even have a job; I'm unsuccessful in that too. Somehow, I have to pay for my car taxes, petrol, and insurance for my car. I always end up getting the money by doing bad things, things I don't like doing.

'Don't stay out too late, Shak. You got to drop Tara off at the doctor's tomorrow,' my mum said while shutting the door behind me. I was going to Majid's house to help him prepare for his wedding day next week.

It was about seven o'clock and I had enough time to make some money. I drove round the corner and phoned Rizwan, my college mate.

'Easy bro, you up for tonight? . . . yeah . . . safe then . . . I meet you there . . .' I spoke to Rizwan as I kept a lookout.

Ten minutes later, Rizwan arrived and we both walked into a petrol station with our hoods up and scarves covering our faces to reveal just our eyes. I had parked my car about two minutes away from the filling station. Rizwan picked up a few things to eat as I was setting myself up to rob the joint. I walked calmly to the counter and reached for my pellet gun. The cashier understood exactly what was about to happen so he slowly opened the cash register and just froze.

'Hurry, man, don't have all day. Give me the money, now.' I pulled out the gun and aimed it directly at his chest.

At this moment, the cashier started sweating like hell and Rizwan stepped in front of the door for a quick exit.

'Come on, I won't shoot ya, just give us the money, man,' I said keenly. The cashier grabbed as many notes as he could and handed them to me.

'Good boy. You should be employee of the month now.' I smiled back under my scarf.

I walked out counting the money. Suddenly the cashier pushed a button under the cash machine to close the automatic doors as a weapon; the glass doors swung shut with full force. Rizwan was about to leave the shop but the glass doors shattered and hard-pressed him out, forcing him to fall on the floor.

'Damn, Riz, get up, man.' I dashed the money in my pocket and lifted Rizwan up; all the things he stole had fallen as well.

'Aarr! Shak, I'm hurt, man. He's callin' the coppers!' Rizwan stood up shakily whilst looking sharply at the cashier. The cashier phoned the police and smiled back at us and then looked at the CCTV camera.

Rizwan and I had picked all the junk food that had fallen and made a run for it. Luckily, I had parked close and out of sight from the petrol station. We got out of breathe by the time we reached the car even though it was quite close. We sat in, silently catching our breath.

'Last time,' Rizwan said as he looked at me.

'Last time, Riz,' I replied as I nodded my head as well.

'You all right? You took a hard fall, man.' I looked at him concerned. Rizwan took of his coat to see if his back was all right, but there was nothing there—no scratches or bruises.

'Nothin man, lucky for your duffel you didn't even get a scratch,' I responded.

'Really, I swear I could feel the door . . . Smack! He he!' Rizwan laughed.

I got the bunch of notes out of my pocket and split it into two and handed half to Rizwan.

'He he, payday, innit, Shak!' Rizwan giggled.

'Yeah, man,' I smiled, looking at the money.

I dropped Rizwan home. It was about half eight then I went to Majid's house. Shazin, Majid's sister, opened the door and said, 'Hey, Shakiel, everything's done for today. Maj, Ali, and Omar are in the living room, Mum and Dad have gone for an early night.'

I walked in.

'Thanks, Shazin,' I said gratefully.

For the past year, I have got to know Shazin a bit more as I have been coming to the house quite a few times due to the preparation of Majid's wedding. According to our parents, I am set up to marry her whenever I feel like it. She's quite pretty and clever, but I don't like her because my eyes are only set on Naila. I only see Naila at weddings. I could see her every day if I drive to her house, but I don't have the guts to. There's also the problem that she is already set up to marry Ali, my other cousin. I've liked her even before I knew Ali was set up with her.

Meanwhile, I said salaams to my cousins and sat down. They were all watching football, Juventus versus Ajax.

'Gangsta, where were you? Your mum phoned an hour ago,' Majid sniggered.

'You know where I was, doing ma ol shifts,' I replied.

'Joker, u gorra stop that one day man,' Majid laughed.

Ali and Omar looked at me confused.

Shazin walked in nudging Majid with her foot. Majid looked at her annoyingly then looked towards me. 'Shak, ma sis wants to speak to ya in the kitchen.'

'Huh? Okay,' I answered. I knew where this was going.

I followed her to the kitchen. I went to get a cup of water.

'Yeah, you know ma mum and dad and your mum want us to get married. I'm not fussed, but when do you plan for the wedding to happen?' she enquired.

'Ar yeah, about that, you really want me, I mean, are you ready? I know I ain't ready at all, Shazin. I'm only nineteen, got no goals in life, don't even know what I'm gonna be doing tomorrow,' I answered while my forehead sweat a little.

'Shak, of course I'm ready . . . I know you want to *too.* Listen, I like you and you like me so what's the problem?' she demanded. At this moment, I was seriously thinking of Naila a lot and didn't want to give any false promises.

'Listen, if you really, really, really wanna get married to a butt-ugly guy like me, with no ambitions in life, then I'll think about it.' I couldn't believe I just said that.

'Yeah, I really wanna, but I don't see what you gorra think about, Shak. All that stuff doesn't bother me the slightest because I know we'll be happy and that's all we need be,' she replied immediately.

'Nah, I mean if you really, really, really, *really* want to get marr . . .'

Shazin cut me off by answering, 'Yes, I really, really, really, really want to get married to you.'

At this moment of time, I thought that there's no way out of this.

'You sure, don't you have a boyfriend or something?'

She looked at me with a shocked expression on her face.

'Shazin, I'm sorry, I didn't mean to say that,' I apologised.

'You don't like me,' Shazin cried.

'Nah, it's not that, it's 'cuz I'm not ready yet,' I responded.

'But you still like me.' Shazin sighed.

She had such a miserable face by now that I had to say, 'Yeah,' just to make her happy.

'You know this is an arranged marriage and not a love one,' I confirmed with Shazin.

'Yeah, I know. Why?' Shazin replied.

'Oh, no reason, just checking,' I said while walking out of the kitchen and back into the living room.

'What were you two chatting about?' Ali spoke.

'Bloody marriage, man,' I replied.

'He he, what you sayin' about ma weddin' next year wiv Naila?' Ali said proudly. Hearing Naila's name by someone else gave electricity to my nerves. Majid automatically looked at me to remind me about Ali and Naila's plans.

'Sounds good. Anyway, Maj, in a few days time, you won't be single anymore, married to Dilly and that, so get high tonight, boy,' Omar said while swiftly changing the subject. Omar passed Majid a spliff and started the session.

'Switch this shibby off; play some Cypress Hill. The CD's already in there,' Majid informed Omar while he took a few drags of the spliff. The tunes started playing and the room started filling up with smoke. Before we knew it, it was eleven o'clock and the boys were out cold. I dazedly got up and left the house to go home. I knew they would get done in the morning by Majid's parents.

I walked in the house, hearing the television on. I strolled into the living room where my mother was sitting watching news, and she hardly stays up this late.

'Mum, what you doing up at this time?' I queried.

'I was worried about you. You weren't at Maj's house and your phone was off,' my mum replied with a tired yawn.

'I went to fill up and my phone's battery died; you don't need to worry,' I made clear while taking my coat off. I noticed the stolen money from inside my jacket pocket and took some out. I handed it to my mum; it looked like a few hundred.

'What? Where are you getting this money? And listen, one day you going to get caught driving with no licence, so apply for it, you understand?' my mum fumingly snapped at me.

'It's an early present and I'll . . . get . . . my licence, don't worry,' I replied.

'Don't worry, don't worry, a mother will never stop worrying for her children. Don't give me that "Don't worry business,"' my mum said while standing up and poking me with her fingers on my chest.

'And another thing, you never speak to me these days. What's wrong? You think I'm old fashioned or something,' she laughed.

'Nah, I do talk to you. I say salaam . . .'

'And that's it. It's just salaam. Something's up. You start smoking again?' my mum finished my sentence.

'No,' I replied with a guilty look.

'You got a girlfriend?' My mum looked at me to see my facial expressions because I think mothers can know things by just looking into your eyes and analysing your reactions when a subject comes up.

'You miss your dad?' My mum then raised her eyebrow to see if that was the problem.

'A bit,' I answered.

My mum noticed that that wasn't the entire problem by my expressions.

'Something else is up, I know it. What is it?' She crossed her arms and tapped her feet.

'Mum, I never speak to you 'cuz you always busy with other things. When you not, you either with Tara or on the phone, and when I do get the chance to chat to you I forget what to say,' I told my excuse while turning around to go upstairs.

'Wait, Shak, that's the first time you talked to me in a long time. Now, tell me what's the issue or issues,' my mum smiled.

'Nothin, I got nothin' to tell you at the moment. Now let me go sleep, I'm whacked.'

I walked upstairs as my mum shook her head. I walked into my sister's room; she was still awake, writing text messages on her phone.

'You all right, T?' I said while opening the door.

'Yeah, where did you go when Mum phoned? Before you come, I got an hour lecture of how to be a traditional daughter-in-law,' Tara said while hiding her phone under her blanket.

'That's good to hear,' I replied.

'Mum goes sumthin' 'bout your wedding and who you gonna marry,' Tara smiled.

'Who? Ar yeah . . . Shazin,' I guessed.

'No, Mum goes the Shazin thing was only a joke. It's a secret, trust me, Shak, you'll like her,' Tara kept me in suspense.

I walked into the room grabbing a teddy bear.

'Tell me, Tara, or I'll rip the bear's head off.'

'Tear it, it's yours from when you were a baby, don't you remember? I ripped all my teddy limbs off when I was a kid, and anyway it's meant to be a surprise,' Tara said while I looked at the teddy bear.

'Go on, tell me. Don't be slack. What does her name begin with?' I begged as I put down the teddy bear.

'Not saying. Listen, Mum's coming. I'm meant to be asleep,' Tara whispered.

'Why didn't mum tell me this?' I looked confused.

'When do you ever chat to mum, Shak? Chat to her and you might find out sooner than you think. She thinks you off the track and you gonna do something stupid cause of that. Chat to her, okay?' she replied whispering.

'Okay, laters then. Tell me in the morning.' I walked out frustrated, thinking about who my mum's set me up with now. I walked in my room, still thinking, got into my bed, still thinking. It cannot be Naila, that's for sure; she's set up with Ali. It isn't Shazin. Tara said it isn't her, so who is it? Half three in the morning and I was still thinking. I had a headache all night just thinking.

CHAPTER 3

'*HICCUP, HICCUP.*'

'Someone's thinking of you, Nay,' Shamala giggled.

'Someone's always thinking of me. I always hiccup,' Naila responded.

It was nine o'clock on a bright summer's morning. Shamala stood up from Naila's bed, switched on the hi-fi, and sat back down saying, 'Nay, you ready for your wedding?'

'Yeah, about that, d'you think Ali's my destiny? I mean, is he the one I'm meant to be with? I got ma doubts,' Naila replied while looking out the window.

'Yeah, he's destined to marry you,' Shamala replied while rolling her eyes.

Naila looked at Shamala then sat on the bed with her while saying, 'I had a strange dream the once, where my grandmother shouts this guy's name out to me three times, but I couldn't hear it because I was too excited about seeing her and asking her where she's been for so long. So I ran to her, but she had gone and I had woken up by then and trust me, she never said, "Ali."'

'Oh, no, you know if a person that's passed away tells you something in a dream is one hundred percent true. Did you hear anything else she said to ya?' Shamala said surprisingly.

'Nah, but I heard an L at the end of the name and the name had two syllables,' Naila said as she got more concerned of what the name was.

'Yeah, Al-li,' Shamala laughed.

'Nah, it weren't Ali, trust me,' Naila giggled.

'Then who? You clearly marrying the wrong person then.' Shamala smiled at Naila.

'What? I can't stop the wedding, my dad will kill me,' Naila replied immediately.

'Naila, listen to me, you're stopping it, okay? Do you even love Ali?' Shamala put her hand on Naila's shoulder.

Naila thought for a moment, replying, 'I don't really know, I don't have any feelings for him. I mean, I don't even care what he's even done today.'

'Whoa, you don't love him, you don't love Ali,' Shamala chuckled in surprise.

'I guess not, Shamala. You know what though? I do love the guy ma grandmother was on about even though I don't know him. It was like she knew where my happiness would lie. I can't explain why though.'

Naila dozed off in her own world whilst Shamala brought her back. 'Listen, Nay, next time you dream of your grandmother again, tell her what the name was again, tell her she was too important to see than knowing what she said at that time.'

'I tried, but just seeing her gets me emotional,' Naila sighed.

'Try again, because dreams like that are rough, you know. You gotta cancel the wedding, Nay,' Shamala explained.

'What? And die the next day by my dad? Forget that, Shamala,' Naila snapped.

'Believe it or not, Nay, a passed-away person in a dream is always saying the truth, and if your grandmother never said Ali then cancel the wedding,' Shamala lectured.

'I understand, but my dad's already sent most the expensive invitations out to most of the families in the UK. He's just got to send the rest back home now, which he will do in a few days time,' Naila cried while moving back to the window.

'Yeah and . . .' Shamala stood up to go by the window as well.

'Yeah and . . . I can't do anything about it, can I?' Naila replied.

'You should have said something sooner,' Shamala said while looking out the window at cars going past.

'I know, but I was just too excited of being a twenty-year-old bride at the time it was getting set,' Naila sighed.

'You're twenty-one now and gonna be twenty-two for the wedding. You getting old,' Shamala nodded while smiling.

'Shut up, *buudie.*' Naila tapped Shamala's arm.

'Who you calling buudie? I ain't twenty-one, buudie,' Shamala replied.

'Whatever.' Naila stopped the play argument.

'You still gotta sort your crap out, buudie.' Shamala laughed again.

Naila thought before saying, 'You know, I think my grandmother said Aneel, but I'm not a hundred percent sure.'

'Aneel, huh? The guy who works at Asda? Yeah, he's Okay, I bet it is him,' Shamala reflected.

'Even if it is him, I can't do jack besides knowing Aneel could have been mine,' Naila believed.

'Nay, Nay, Nay, destiny has something to do with the number three, right? And your grandmother told you a name three times, right? So it clearly states that Aneel or whoever is destined for you, so as I was saying, cancel the wedding. Be at least eighty percent sure it's him and marry that person rather than marrying someone you not destined for, Okay?'

'Yeah, Shamala, easier said than done. You forgetting something. My dad and Ali's hands round my neck if I disappoint them at all.' Naila crossed her arms while sitting on the bed again.

Naila was being called from downstairs so both Shamala and Naila went down to perceive what Naila was being called for.

'Naila, baby, go make one cup of *chai* for me. You going to be good daughter-in-law to Ali's family,' Naila's dad said while looking over his shoulder to Naila.

'Okay, dad. Can you drop Shamala off at hers later?' Naila nodded her head to say, 'See what I mean.'

'What? Shamala, you want to go home so early?' Naila's dad looked back to see Shamala.

'No, Uncle, but I got things to do at home so can you drop me off at about twelve?' Shamala said worryingly.

'Don't worry, Shamala, I'll take you. You getting more pretty every time I see you. You making me look ugly, you know?' Naila's dad smiled as Naila and Shamala went in the kitchen to make the tea as well as seeing Naila's mum.

'Mum, you gonna miss me when I'm gone.' Naila got a teabag out of the box of teabags.

'No, I'll appreciate the lack of noise in the house,' Naila's mum joked.

'*Mum,* you're slack,' Naila cried as she poured water into the kettle from the tap.

'You know, Naila, I don't like this Ali guy. He seems to me like a street boy, you know, involved with guns and drugs and all that, but your dad sees something else in him,' Naila's mum said as Naila turned her head to face her mum whilst overflowing the water into the kettle.

'Do you like him?' Naila's mum asked.

Naila froze then stuttered, 'Er . . . yeah, I mean no. I mean . . . er . . . I don't know . . . Mum, I'm only getting married to him because of Dad so I have to like him, innit.'

'You were just like me, Naila, confused, lost. Do you feel like that? Well, that's how arranged marriages go, he he. If I go one step cross the line, I get an ear full from him and the in-laws, but I been a good daughter-in-law. Look, I'm still here . . . I last saw my mum a few years ago and remember thinking on my wedding day that I'll see her ever so often, but I end up seeing her after every few years. I hardly see her and I don't like that, so I'm telling you now I'll be here for you anytime, even if your dad doesn't want you in the house. I'll be here for you, and you have to make it a big deal to see me, okay?' Naila's mum sighed.

'Juldie with the chai!' Naila's dad shouted from the other room.

Naila bought the tea into the other room on a tray, gave it to her dad who was still sitting by the TV, and walked outside with Shamala and her mum. Naila's dad had told Naila's mum to drop Shamala off at her house. She was really annoyed at him.

All three of them sat in the car; Shamala sat at the back with some food to give her parents from Naila's family. The weather had dimmed out since the morning. It was about ten thirty by the time the car started after jerking out a few times.

'So, Mum, who do you think's right for me then?' Naila made conversation to break the silence.

'As I said, I don't like that Ali guy. I think, er . . . What's that young man's name? He's a bit young for you, but he's such a nice boy. What's his name?' Naila's mum was thinking. Naila was so tense as she looked into the centre mirror, eyeing Shamala dead in her eyes. 'Tara's older brother, what's his name? Ar yeah, Shak, yeah, Shakiel.'

As Naila's mum said the name, Naila was stunned as if she figured something out but she didn't say anything.

'Shakiel is such a nice-looking boy. If you were a year or two younger, I would have set you up with him, but don't worry. Things will work out with you and Ali, inshallah.'

Naila was gobsmacked. Naila's mum stopped at traffic lights and saw Naila's reaction.

'What? Was it something I said?' Naila's mum said confusingly.

'What name did you just say?' Naila asked.

'Shakiel. Why?' Naila's mum replied while moving off from the traffic lights.

'Doesn't matter. I thought I just saw someone,' Naila lied.

Naila's mum parked and Shamala jumped out smiling at Naila and saying, 'Salaams, jazakallah for dropping me off, Aunty.' Naila's mum replied with, 'It's okay, salaams.'

She then looked at Naila and asked, 'You all right? You seem strange today.'

'Yeah, I'm Okay, Mum, just got the hiccups,' Naila replied.

Naila's mum drove back detailing Naila on how to cook the tastiest lasagne, but Naila's head was up in the clouds thinking about the boy her mum had just mentioned, but her chatty mum did not notice as they arrived back home.

CHAPTER 4

IT WAS THE wedding of Majid and Dilshad today. I woke up bright and early to make my morning prayer. I've made it a habit to perform *fajr* every morning without fail. If I accidently forget to pray it or pray it late, my day tends to go wrong so I always start my day with the Lord's name in prayer. I prayed especially to see Naila and for Naila to talk to me because I knew if I was to see her I'd be too shy to talk.

I dressed up smart, wearing a three-piece suit and leather shoes: suited and booted. I drove to the petrol station to get petrol and wash my car; it was looking embarrassing to drive in. I went to go pay ten pounds and four pence (I got distracted plus the petrol in the pumps comes out too fast) to the cashier. I picked up a newspaper, seeing a heading reading 'Yet Another Robbery in Sparkhill' with a detailed article about three masked thieves robbing a filling station,' then my phone rang. It was my mum telling me to pick up my sister to get her hair done at a hairdresser. I paid the cashier, putting the paper back down, jumped back in my car thinking of how close Rizwan and I were the other day—we took our other friend, Jason, with us last time, and we're finally making the papers.

I drove home; it was about nine thirty when I reached the house. The wedding was at twelve and my sister decided to do her hair now, today, just before the wedding. Clever, isn't she? I beeped my horn, also noticing that visitors had come from London. It was too late for me to greet them because I had to pick up Omar and his mum as well as take Tara to the hairdressers. So as soon as Tara jumped in the car, I put my foot on the gas and went. It was a ten-minute drive to the hairdressers so I thought, Shall I tell Tara about Naila and ask if she's the one our mum's set me up with? But every time I was about to speak, my mouth dried up and nothing came out of it.

'Mum goes you gotta pick up Omar and his mum,' Tara finally spoke, to break the silence.

'Yeah, I know. Doesn't he have a flippin' car? They got like three cars: his dad's, his mum's and his own, but *nooo* they gorra be picked up. His family's a joke,' I said in anger.

'Chill, Shak, they just live up the road,' Tara indicated as she pointed up the road.

'Okay, whatever.' I kissed my teeth.

'Shak, just here.' Tara pointed at the hairdressers then said, 'If it makes you feel better, your car looks pretty clean today.'

'Thanks. Listen, how long you gonna be?' I said while parking the car.

'Ar, about fifteen minutes, not that long,' Tara replied.

'You best be. I'm gonna be back by then. I'm just gonna go pick them up,' I said as Tara left the car. I hate it when I got missions to do and there's a deadline line to do it all, because not everyone's on my pace.

I picked up Omar and his mum from their house and drove back to the hairdressers. As I waited, I spoke to Omar's mum. 'So Aunty, what's new? You still getting the kitchen done, fitting the laminated lino?'

'Shakiel, I done that ages ago. It shows that you haven't come down my house in a long time. I mean, that got done last year some time. Anyway, how's your mum and sister keeping?' Omar's mum questioned.

'They Okay. My mum's getting on with life, lecturing us about how things should be done and how they were done in her time, and Tara, Tara's still getting me into trouble. She needs help big time.'

Omar's mum laughed. 'Omar got a new phone. It's got a camera, plays fil-lams and plays three MPs.'

'It's called MP3, Mum, not whatever you said.' Omar shook his head at his mum while smiling.

I looked at my watch and it was eleven o'clock. 'Damn, what the hell's Tara playing at? It eleven, we going to be late for the wedding.' I furiously beeped my horn and pressed the gas pedal down to let it roar. Suddenly, Tara looked outside from the hairdresser's window as did the girls who were having their hair done.

Tara walked outside from the hairdressers with a drop-dead hairdo, but I was more bothered about her taking the mick. She jumped in saying, 'At last! I been waiting for time.'

'What you on about? I been waiting here for forty-five minutes. Didn't you bother looking out the window?' I shouted.

'My hair was done in twenty minutes and then I started chatting to the girls,' Tara said while fastening her belt.

That took me over the edge. 'You flippin' joke, didn't you see me outside? Is my car invisible now, you blind—?'

'Soz, Shak,' Tara apologised.

'Trust me, T, if you were a guy, I would have knocked some sense into ya by now. You act so stupid sometimes.' I punched the horn, making it beep.

'Shak, you knock me out anyway,' Tara cried.

'No, I don't though!' I shouted while punching the horn again, creating an even longer beep.

'Okay, that's all, both of you. Thank God I never had a second child.' Omar's mum intercepted our arguing.

'See what I mean? She gets me into trouble all the bloody time.' I calmed down a little.

'It's cause you love her so much, you fight with her. She fights with you because she lo . . .' Omar concluded the argument but both Tara and I finished his sentence with a 'No way!'

I drove home in silence to go pick my mum up. My mum had set the alarm, shut the house door, was all dressed up, and was waiting outside.

'Where were you for so long?' my mum asked.

'Don't ask, Mum, let's just say Tara,' I replied.

'I don't even wanna know,' my mum said as Tara sat in the back so my mum could sit in the front.

'Is everything okay with the house?' my mum asked Omar's mum.

'Yeah,' Omar's mum responded.

'Okay, visitors have gone, thank God. Now let's go,' my mum said in gratitude.

As I reversed, I looked back to see if any cars were coming, I saw three squashed people in the back seat and then laughed out, 'I remember when I was one of you.'

The *nikkah* was for about twenty minutes; Dilshad's older brother gave a speech. 'Thank you, everyone who's come. Some of us have come from different cities around the UK, and some from different countries around the world, and I just want to say a big thank you for making the effort of coming. Now, food will be served so if all the ladies can go to the main hall here and the men in the hall opposite.' He located the eating halls to the ladies and men. Slowly, the ladies went to go eat whilst the men went to congratulate Majid.

During the Nikkah, I was trying to spot Naila, but I could only see her mum and dad. I felt disappointed and let down. After I congratulated Majid, I went to the ladies' dining hall and served them for a while just to see if Naila was there, but she wasn't. So I left and went outside behind the building with my cousins Omar, Ali, Riaz, Zain, and Aktar who where persuading my cousin, Riaz, to let them see who he was texting under the table while the Nikkah was going on. As soon as Riaz saw me, he immediately put his phone away. I was surprised why he put it away so quickly, but I wasn't that bothered to find out.

'Yes, Shak, Riaz got a girl but don't wanna show us. He was texting for time when the *molana* was saying all that stuff. I read something like he's gonna meet up with her in a bit, here.' Omar filled me in with the story.

'So . . . has anyone turned up?' I replied just for the sake of it.

'Nah, just those kids there with Shamala.' Zain pointed at one of Naila's first cousins who was playing with her younger sister and niece. I instantly thought, *Shamala will know if Naila's here because she always stays with her during the summer holidays.*

'I'll go ask Shamala if she's the one he's texting.' I walked towards her while my cousins looked at me.

I don't really know Shamala that well so it was a bit awkward asking her about Naila's whereabouts. 'Easy Shamala, how's life?' I broke a sweat.

'All right, how's your mum and sister?' she answered. That's always the reply I get: "How's your mum and sis?" Not "How are you doing?"

'Yeah, they okay. Chillin' most of the time. Anyways, what I was gonna say was, don't you chill with Naila anymore? I mean, I haven't seen you with her lately.' I swallowed my saliva. It was really difficult for me to say her name aloud as well as talking to Shamala, who is quite pretty herself.

'Nah, we still chat. I was at hers a few nights ago. She didn't come today 'cuz she told me that she didn't want to because . . .' Shamala nearly spilt the beans about what Naila's mum told Naila who she thought Naila should be with. Shamala looked at me head to toe, then said, 'Err, she didn't wanna miss *Eastie (EastEnders).*'

'Huh, never mind, err. You got a fing going wiv Riaz or wot?' I asked her.

'Ew, no way. Who told you that?' Shamala looked at me in disgust.

'Never mind, Shamala, safe then,' I replied while walking off to my cousins.

My cousins were watching us but could not hear the conversation that Shamala and I had and were eager to hear what was said.

'No, she ain't the one.' I took them out their misery. I wasn't really bothered about who Riaz was chatting to until I heard Riaz confessing she lives here, in the Mid West. This limited the number of girls down to a few that was in his age range.

Ali grabbed for Riaz's phone but Riaz rapidly deleted all his received messages. 'Chill man. You'll find out when the time comes, just like everyone else, you get me?' Riaz snatched his phone back of Ali and gave us a cheeky smile.

Two hours later, the photos with the bride and groom were taking place; I had just finished eating with the latecomers as I went in to serve again. I was thinking about what Shamala was about to say, because she tried not saying something to me. I was thinking when I was eating that Naila must not be meant for me because I pray to see her so much, but it don't happen. Instead, I see Shazin more than often, so I got to stop dreaming and get back to reality because Naila is Ali's girl and Shazin, well, Shazin is, I think, meant for me. Destiny is playing a rough game with my heart and I keep losing this game, and the only time I can win is if I get linked up with Shazin, which isn't fair but that's just the way it goes, I guess.

It seemed like everyone was enjoying themselves; a few people started leaving because everything was finished. I was talking to my uncle, who was telling me what his plans are for the future. He always seems to tell me the same thing but doesn't go on to do it. My mum interrupted by saying she wanted to go home, so I said to my uncle, 'Inshallah, your plans will work out some day. Okay, salaams then.' waving walked off and waved my hand.

'Yeah, one day, okay, bye then,' my uncle replied.

Majid and Dilshad were also leaving to go back to his house. They looked very happy together, like they going to have a very fun time with each other's company. It was nice seeing all my relatives after a (school) year of hard work, but it's a shame I didn't see Naila. I wonder why she didn't come. I wonder what she's doing at this very moment.

CHAPTER 5

THE NEXT DAY, my mum told me to go to town to get a camera she had ordered a month back. I went with Tara by bus because the parking in town is really expensive.

'You know anything about the Riaz situation?' I said while sitting down by the window.

'Huh, wh . . . what situation?' Tara hesitated.

'He's chatting crap to this next gal here in the Mid West,' I replied.

'Nah, Riaz, is an all right guy. I was chat . . . speaking to him on MSN Messenger a few days ago. How's he related to us, Shak?' Tara asked.

I looked outside the window and thought for a bit. 'He's our . . . er . . . he's Dad's cousin's uncle's daughter's son. Why?'

'I just wanted to know.'

We stopped talking after that because Tara received a text from someone and she was replying a long text back.

We finally reached town centre and got off the bus. Town was quite busy, considering it was a late Monday morning. My mum told me that town is getting rough; she saw a few fights going off on the news so that's why I had to look after Tara even though she's seventeen.

'Where the hell are the police when all this goes on?' my mum says. 'Why do we pay taxes?'

'Come, Argos is this way, come, Tara.' I told Tara to follow me, as she was still texting while coming off the bus. I wondered who she was texting. We started walking to the store, passing pretty Muslim girls; I put my head down for two reasons: my sister was watching me and because I thought of Naila and surprisingly Shazin as well.

We walked into the Argos store and Tara went to go pick up the camera while I sat down on a sofa that was on for show. She was in the queue for about twenty minutes, which took the mick. I phoned my uncle, because I remembered he worked just up High Street. 'Yeah, salaams, bro . . . You working today? . . . Yeah . . . I'm with Tara at Argos. I'll pop down after, got nufin else to do . . . Yeah, okay, sef then . . . salaams then, bro.'

After ten boring minutes, Tara returned with the good. I told her that we visiting my uncle at his workplace, so we did. Town was getting busier by the minute. We got to my uncle's workplace and Tara met up with her friends. So I went in and started talking to my uncle as Tara stood outside with her friends. Time passed on until Tara came in and gave salaam to our uncle and told me that she was getting a lift with her friends so she gave me the camera. Five minutes after she left, I decided to head off too.

I walked out with the camera really close to me, thinking some punk might jump me for it because my uncle reminded me that the city is getting rough and these days thieves don't care who's looking. I started walking towards the bus stop, which was about five hundred yards away, holding the camera. Suddenly, this one punk grabbed me from behind. My heart started pounding, I got a tight grip of the Argos bag and then started shaking the muppet off. I successfully got him off, then I turned round and booted the son-of-a-gun to the ground.

'Shakiel, man, you winded me, you prick,' the thief squeaked out. I looked carefully and it was my old friend from secondary school who was really finding it difficult to breathe. I reached out my hand to pick him up. 'Oh, shibby, Saj, is that you, bro? Soz, man. Oh no, I thought you gonna tabax me, bro.'

Saj got up then gently punched my arm, then started laughing. 'I feel sorry for someone who does jack ya, man. You gone tall and stronger. Last time I seen ya, bro, you were this high and you weren't no fighter.' Saj put his hands to his chest to show how tall I was. I laughed.

'How you been, bro? Long time no see. I heard your parents hooked you up with a phat ride and that.' I dusted Saj's top.

He replied, 'Yeah, man, for ma twentieth birthday party. I sold ma banger to ma 'cuz. He bought it for two tons. He's only sixteen but he can rip that ride silly. Ma mum and dad got me a Nissan Pulsar. Sick ride, bro, sick ride.'

'True, bro. You seen anyone else from our ol' school? I ain't seen no one,' I said while I started walking to the bus stop with him.

'I ain't seen no one either . . . Nah, I'm lyin. I seen Shoiab. He was at the tracks one day. He got a gal and a kid, dunno if they married though, bro. There's a link up soon, with just us boys from school. You should land. It's at a lounge in Moseley. Anyway, ma car's parked up there, so see ya when I see ya. I'll ding you the details of that link up. You still got ma number, yeah?' Saj pointed to the car park.

'Yeah, yeah, I still got your number. I'll try pop down, safe then, bro,' I responded as I shook his hand and walked to the bus stop. I hadn't seen those guys in ages so I thought I might link them up.

It started raining and I was a bit hungry so I went into a nearby shop for shelter. Instead, I went and bought some snacks and had come out quickly because there were a lot of people coming in due to the rain. I put my hood up and stood at the queue of the bus stop. I put my earphones in and played my MP3 player and waited and waited.

Fifteen minutes later, the bus finally came and the bus queue was so long, I couldn't even see the last person,. The doors of the bus opened and the people had come off and the people waiting were jumping on, but then I heard banging and swearing. I looked forward and I saw a bunch of black guys fighting to get in. The bus driver obviously closed the door, preventing them to go on. A lot of moaning started from the queue when the bus driver drove off, leaving the rest of us. The black guys started getting mad and were swearing at the innocent people waiting. The black guys walked off frustrated back into the shopping mall.

I was soaking wet, cold, and hungry; I had eaten all my snacks quite a while back. Another bus came ten minutes later; I heard a lot of 'At last!' from the people waiting in front of me. The people who were on the bus came off and the people waiting jumped on. I starting walking forward, feeling drained.

'You aite, Shak?' someone said while I walked towards the bus with a soft and warm voice. I looked up to see who it was then looked back down because of the rain. Oh, no! No way! I took my hood off and gently replied, 'Yeah, you okay?' I could not believe my eyes. It was Naila.

A glow of a bright light shone on her due to the lights of the shop behind her being switched on. *What do I say? What do I do? Shall I catch the bus or go with her? Shall I catch the bloody bus that I have been waiting for ages or go with her? Damn!* She raised her eyebrows and smiled before walking off.

Damn!

I looked back, but all I could see was the back of her getting farther and farther away. I didn't know what to do; I was holding the queue now. I jumped on the bus thinking she was much better than I thought.

Thoughts filled my mind rapidly while looking out the window. I hadn't seen her for ages. Are my *duas* coming true? Is she noticing me? Was that really her? It wasn't a dream. I started having a funny shiver feeling but loved it. It was the butterflies going crazy inside me.

I got off the bus feeling like I was on top of the world, smiling and laughing for no reason at people I didn't even know. I took out my wallet from my back pocket and slipped out the picture I had of her. It had folded accidentally and had a few creases. I didn't care; I dusted it and looked at it for about ten seconds until I nearly walked into a lamppost.

At home, my mum was cooking, my sister was watching TV, and I was on the phone to my cousin, Majid, telling him who I had just met. I fibbed most of it. I got the camera out of the bag and gave it to my mum, who said thank-you in a whisper due to me being on the phone. Majid sounded like he wasn't bothered as much as I was, because he knew she was set up with Ali and I couldn't do anything about that. Ali is a safe guy to some. It's just that he got the girl I want, which instantly makes me jealous of him, which therefore makes me dislike him.

I say my salaams and have conversations with the guy, but he's not a close friend that I would just chill with. My other cousins love the geezer and want him to go everywhere they go, but I leave it as it is. A few years back, Ali and I had a collision; it was at his sister's birthday party—mainly girls turned up as well as close family. The tension was there with me but Ali was calm; he had just sweet-talked his way into making me carry all the barbeque equipment into the garden, which weighed a bloody ton at the time. Ali had just started liking Naila, but I had no idea he did. When

I took the grill out, I was waiting for him outside to bash him with it. My dad was still alive. He saw that I wanted to hit him, but he surprisingly didn't do anything about it. My sister Tara wanted him to get it as well, as Ali didn't let Tara be a part of the present opening. So, Tara was the one who told Ali to go outside. I was ready with the grill, and as he stepped out, *smack!* I smacked the grill on his forehead and he banged his head off the door, which cut his forehead slightly. He got vexed and swore at me a couple of times. I had done the one thing I really wanted to do that day; I will always remember that for the rest of my life, and I loved it. I lifted the grill up again and told my sister, 'Shall I do it again?' Tara said, 'Yeah, go on, Shak.'

'Yo, Ali, this is from my sister.' I laid it down again. *Smack!* On his head again, making him go unconscious. I was kicked out of the house and was told to never step foot in their house again, but I went in the next day to apologise. My parents forced me to.

I went to the mosque later on to pray *magrib* because I had to thank the Lord for that special little moment he just blessed me with. My friends Asif and Mohammad were waiting outside for me.

'Salaams, bro, long time no see. Where you been hiding, bro? You getting weak.' Asif shook my hands.

'Been busy with things, you get me?' I replied.

'Salaams, Shak, you wanna do us a favour bro?' Mohammad shook my hands too. I looked at both of them, knowing what they would ask of me.

'You gonna come on jamaat wiv us? All of us are going: me, Asif, Nav, Hussien, Asad, and them boys, bare of us are going,' Mohammad said while walking down with Asif and me.

'You know me, bro. I'm up for it if ma mum's aite wiv it.'

'Remember when we used to go wiv Ansar and that? We used to have a mad laugh, man. I miss that geezer, man.' Asif looked to the skies and shook his head.

'Yeah, man, big time,' both Mohammad and I responded.

'Look, Ansar would've wanted you to go wiv us. He knew this deen was the right thing to be a part of.' Asif tried persuading me to join them.

'Geezer, I told ya, if my mum allows me to go, then I'll land,' I replied.

Jamaat was all right, it was just a long thing that took away our weekend, even though we'd have nothing planned for the weekend; it was still something I didn't want to be doing. I always dropped the "need to ask my mum" as an excuse because I knew my mother didn't like the idea of going on jamaat so she'd disagree with me going. I wouldn't go if I didn't want to.

CHAPTER 6

A FEW WEEKS later, about eleven o'clock in the morning, my phone rang. It was Rizwan. He told me that he saw my sister with another guy.

'So, wot's the sketch, man? Shall we do him over or wot man?' Rizwan suggested.

I couldn't think properly. Bad thoughts were just rushing through my mind. I felt like I wanted to kill this joker. Rizwan never told me who it was or where they were, I just simply said, 'Sort this punk bitch out, yeah.' I was exploding inside but I knew Rizwan would deal with it.

Two o'clock on the dot, at the Shawarma Palace, a restaurant in a Muslim-populated area. Tara and Riaz had just ordered their meals. 'Does your bro know 'bout me and you, T?' Riaz poured a glass of water for himself then Tara.

'Na, not yet. He might not understand straight away. Give me time . . . Guess who's popular today. Those guys are calling ya outside. Do you know 'em?' Tara pointed outside to some thugs who were trying to call Tara to call Riaz to go outside.

Riaz looked outside and looked confused because he didn't know them at all. He told Tara he would be back in a bit and walked out the restaurant. Riaz's heart started pounding. 'Yeah, can I help you?' said Riaz while trembling inside. There were three thugs, one wore all black and a bandana covering his nose and mouth, another wore a long leather jacket with a baseball cap, and the last one wore a black duffel coat with the hood up.

'Yeah, man, you can help me. I think you parked your car in front of mine,' smiled out the one with the baseball cap. He was gripping Riaz's shirt.

'I think there's some misunderstanding, lads. I don't drive. Actually I'm only seventeen. I'm not allowed to drive, or am I?' Riaz knew what was coming for him so he tried his best to talk his way out of it, but it was as though they weren't even listening. Riaz tried to make a run for it but the thug who was gripping him held him tighter.

'You ain't goin' nowhere, prick. Give us all you got and we won't beat the crap out of you,' the thug with the hoody threatened. Riaz started crying, 'Please, brother, don't hurt me. I'm on a date and . . . and plus I don't have nothing. The girl's paying.'

'Wot thaaf, this guy's a pussy boy. He makes the girl pay. Let's do double the damage, boys.'

The thug with the bandana shoved Riaz to a car, then *boom!* He punched his face and Riaz dropped to the ground.

All three of them started kicking the hell out of him while he helplessly lay on the floor, crying.

The thug with the hoody lifted him up by the collar, ripping it as well. 'Let's have some fun, boys. No one's seen us.' He then started jabbing his stomach and smacked his face. The others followed by putting their fists up and hopping around him and punching him down like a punching bag.

Minutes later, Tara had walked out to look for Riaz; she walked in the car park and saw Riaz on the floor. She screamed.

The thug with the baseball cap saw Riaz trying to get up then took a knuckle-duster from the inside of his leather jacket and *bang!*

Half past two, my phone rang. It was Rizwan again. 'Sorted, bro.'

I smiled.

The thugs legged it quick time as soon as people started turning up due to Tara's screaming. Riaz was bleeding a lot and was also unconscious. Blood was all over the place. Bruises from head to toe. Riaz was knocked out cold. Tara was crying as she took off his jacket and covered him. The public crowded the scene.

Twenty minutes later, an ambulance came. Someone who was around had phoned for one. The paramedics took Riaz and told Tara she couldn't go with them.

Tara's tears dried up. She didn't know what to do, where to go, who to tell. She caught the bus home and went in her room straight away.

I could tell something was up as I opened the door to her room. I felt bad. I didn't like seeing her like that, but I didn't want any fools getting with my sister, and especially behind my back. In my house, I run things. Actually my mum does, but I'm the man of the yard.

Quarter to nine, Tara's phone rang. It was Riaz. 'You all right, Tara? Did you get hurt?'

'I'm aite. How the hell are you? I'm sorry, Riaz. I didn't know they would do that to you. Where are you now?' Tara started crying again.

'I'm okay, thankfully. I just got a few bumps and bruises and got a few bad cuts on my face. I think one of them had a tool or something and hit me with it. I'm outside of the hospital. My parents are here as well. Don't worry. I told them I was just getting something from the shops and got mugged. I didn't say anything about you.'

He paused. 'It's so good hearing your voice, you know . . . I think I owed someone money or something back in the day, but at least the worst is over. They took all my money. What did . . . Did you have to pay? I'll pay you . . .'

'Shut up, Riaz,' Tara laughed. 'I missed straight away so no one paid, but forget about that. I really thought I never see you again.'

'I . . . I phoned a few people before I rang you to sort this out for good. I think I know who done me over.'

Tara thought for a minute, *It can't be Shakiel; he doesn't know anything about this, or does he?*

'I think it was someone from my secondary school. I really needed bus fare so I borrowed it of this guy called Azam and forgot to pay him back. So I've told my college friends to pay him a visit later on today,' Riaz told Tara.

'Don't let them do something stupid, Riaz,' Tara said.

Knock knock. A bunch of black guys knocked on a door.

'Hey, I think you got the wrong yard, boys,' a guy said as he looked through the door's eyehole and then opened the door.

'You Azam?' the black guy in the centre said.

'I got something for ya.' Azam thought he would get jumped or shot as the black guy was taking something out of his jeans pocket.

It was small, and the guy struggled to find it. 'Oh, here it is. It's fifty pence.'

'Thank you.'

The black guy handed over a fifty-pence coin to Azam and Azam took it, looking confused.

'Oh, the person who sent the money also sent this.' The gang was about to turn around and go, then the one in the centre turned around and gave Azam a note.

'Thanks, guys,' Azam said. Then he read the note.

Azam, my Science class buddy, I realise I haven't seen you since we left school last year and I owed you some money. I have sent you the payment via delivery with my close college colleagues, hope they did not scare you in the process. I understand how frustrated you might be with the late payment but there was no need to get me mugged. I was on a date with the most gorgeous girl I've ever seen so it was very inappropriate. I forgive you for the incident. If you were wondering by any chance, I am okay. I have been treated and will be on my feet real soon. Apologies for any misunderstanding. Take care. Accept this as a receipt of my repayment.

Riaz.

Ten o'clock, Riaz's phone rang in the hospital. Patients and nurses turned to him and looked angry.

'Sorry,' Riaz whispered as he pressed *answer* on his phone.

'Yo, Riaz, job done.' It was one of his college friends.

'Thanks, lads. I owe you a big one.'

My mum was still downstairs watching an Asian drama. I was on the laptop on MSN and Tara was still in her room. I think she was sleeping now.

'Mum, do you dream of Dad still?' I said.

'Shakiel, I can't get the man out of my mind,' my mum smiled. 'I do still dream of him and I do still miss him a lot. The last dream I had of him was about a week ago now. He told me that . . . we were in the garden, right, he told me, "I'm missing all of you so much, where I am. I can never leave it, but if you need me, I'm there. Make sure you don't leave the kids for one second. They need us more than they've needed us before. Don't worry about me." And I'm saying, "I'm missing you so so much. I need you, I want you, please don't go. I'm all alone without you." And then all your dad said was, "With Allah, you can never be lonely."

'In the dream, tears were coming in my eyes so much, my eyes were blurry. He left us so young, Shakiel. Promise me this: You will always look out for us both, your sister and I. I will always look out for you both, always will, always have, because I'm your mother. And also keep your deen strong in your life. I know what I've said about going out on those jamaats, but your dad used to go and it changed him so much, so always keep your deen strong.'

'I will, Mum, always,' I replied with a watery grin. I always want to hug my mother but I never do, and I felt like I had to at this moment so I reached out to hug her. She looked so shocked but let me hug her. She wept out a little more saying, 'Thank you, Shakiel.'

I stayed downstairs for another ten minutes then went up to sleep. As I walked up, I looked at Tara's bedroom door and thought, *Shall I check up on her?* I slowly opened the door and crept in.

Tara had fallen asleep while sitting on the edge of her bed. I felt bad. I opened the bed sheet and pushed her to sleep. I don't usually touch her at all, but on this occasion I didn't mind. As I laid her down, I noticed her sleeves were wet with her tears. At this moment, I covered her with the bed sheet and thought, *I should not have done what I done. There easily could have been another way of sorting it. I'm such an idiot, man.*

CHAPTER 7

IT WAS A slow, warm, Friday afternoon. The supermarket store was closing at half four and Naila's shift was about to finish. Naila had one last customer at her till.

'So, you gonna do anything special tonight,' the customer asked while packing her groceries.

'Hmmm, maybe not. Got no plans to do anything, but who knows? I might treat myself to a Fruit & Nut Dairy Milk slab.' Naila giggled while registering her last fruit bag. 'Why do you ask?'

'Just wanted to know. You look like the type who loves partying with friends and family, you so good looking, you know.' The customer picked up her bags and admired Naila's beauty.

Naila blushed and said, 'Na, I don't party, I'm a homegirl but thanks about the compliment. Yeah, I'm more in the kitchen, helping Mum out, than clubbing and stuff.' Naila waved her goodbye then switched of her till.

Naila put on her jacket and then remembered her mother wanted some bread so she went to the bread isle and picked up some bread where her manager was. 'Hey, Rose, you here till late tonight. I'm just finishing, just picking up Mum's stuff before I go.'

'Yeah, you know how it is, got to clean up after everyone. Oh, Naila, how's wedding preps going for you?' Rose enquired.

'It's okay. It's all out of my hands now, my family have totally took over everything, but it's okay. I like seeing them happy.' Naila sighed.

'That's nice, hope everything goes well for you and him and hope you have a nice evening. See you tomorrow.' Rose neatened up the presentation of a few goods in front of her.

'Yeah, see you tomorrow, Rose. I'm off now, bye bye,' Naila told Rose as she went to pay for the bread and then left the store.

While walking to the bus stop, she saw the bus coming. Naila started running, thinking the bus would not stop due to no one being there. But she knew she wouldn't make it so she slowed down.

The bus went past the bus stop. Naila sighed again as she just arrived as the bus went past. The bus stopped a few metres past the stop. A man walked out in a dark jacket. Naila had already realised the bus had stopped and ran to it immediately. The man saw her running and told the bus driver to wait. Naila looked at the man to say thank-you before realising it was her uncle who was married to my mother's sister.

'Thanks . . . Salaams, Uncle Tarik.' She thanked him while jumping onto the bus. Uncle Tarik looked at Naila and smiled.

Uncle Tarik is dumb. He cannot talk, actually he cannot speak properly. He makes sounds like it's coming out of his nose. Everyone feels sorry for him but he hates people sympathising and thinking he can't do anything by himself. He can do everything by himself, actually he does everything by himself. Besides, when we have parties or weddings the elders always make sure someone helps him out with each and everything he does. His wife, my aunty, does everything she should for a husband but does not look at him as a disabled person and treats him normally.

Naila sat down in the bus and looked outside the window wondering when she last had seen Uncle Tarik. *It was at the wedding last month, wasn't it? No wait, he didn't come to it. Where was the last time I met him? Oh, yeah, it was at that house party a few years back, at Nasim's. No, it wasn't. It was Tara's. Yeah, that's right, Tara's. I haven't seen Tara for quite a long time now. Actually, I haven't seen any of them.*

Naila crossed her legs and put her hand on her chin and then went back into deep thought. *Hey, I just met her elder brother last week, yeah, he looked like he was in a hurry. I wonder where he was going. He he. Shakiel.* (Naila uncrossed her legs then looked outside the window again.) *Shakiel, he's the one my grandmother was on about and Shamala was telling me about him at that last wedding that he was asking about me. It was Shakiel all along. My grandmother was saying* Shak-iel, *duh!'*

As soon as Naila got home, she rang Shamala and said, 'Shamz, it's Shakiel. It was Shakiel all along . . . Of course I'm sure, Shamala.' Naila laughed and giggled. 'My grandmother was saying Shakiel.' Shamala laughed again. 'What do you mean, cancel the wedding for defo . . . I can't . . . I know I have to, but I can't . . . Yeah . . . Yeah, you know something? Since that dream, Shamala, I've grown to love the person my grandmother was telling me about. At first, it was something like *yeah, whatever,* then it was like *he is meant for me, no matter what he's like, even though I didn't know who it was all these years.* I liked him, then like-liked him, then obviously I started to love him after that . . . I know I didn't tell you this before, it was because I wasn't sure if it was real. But now I'm sure sure . . . Yeah I'm sure . . . Yeah, double positive . . . I'm gonna go down and look ma dad in the eyes and tell him the truth, and if he says, "I don't care," I'm walking back upstairs and phoning you again to tell you how mean my dad was. Okay . . . Okay, see ya.'

Naila put the phone down and took a deep breath, opened her door, and walked out slowly. Naila started to sweat and was getting cold feet. She thought for a minute to forget about it and just go back into her room but stamped her foot down and said to herself, 'I'm doing it.'

Naila's dad was fixing a broken table leg in the dining room.

'Dad, can . . . can I speak to you?' Naila stuttered.

'You know you can tell me anything, Nay Nay,' her dad answered whilst holding the three-legged table up. He had his back facing her, which made it easier for Naila to tell him.

'You know, about Ali and the wedding, don't you think, err, it's a bit too early for me?' Naila was gripping her hands so tight from behind her, not even her sweat on her palms could slip them apart.

'I thought you wanted to get married to him.' Naila's dad turned around to look at her. 'You do know most the preparations are done and I have already sent some of the invitations out. I wouldn't have if you didn't want me to.'

Her dad's tone was changing. Naila started getting scared. 'I . . . I wanted to but never had an in-depth thought of what I'm about to get myself into.' Naila's body language was as though she was about to faint because her dad was looking at her furiously and also breaking the third table leg with his bare hands.

'You want me to call it off, huh? Is that what you want me to do?' The table leg that he broke off was about to snap into two like a pencil in his hand.

'Err . . . Ye . . . Yeah, please, but if you don't want to, it's okay,' Naila squeaked out.

'Okay . . .'

Naila looked relieved.

But he continued. 'Okay, you answered me, that's good. Now I'm thinking, still thinking, my answer is no!' Naila's dad broke the table leg and the table fell down as her dad moved away. 'You are going to your wedding whether you like it or not. Wait. There must be a reason why you don't want to get married. You don't want to marry Ali, isn't it?' He moved closer to Naila as she moved away from her angry dad. 'Who's the one you want to marry, huh Naila? Your mum told me that or hinted out that something's wrong with Ali. *Is there?'* her dad roared out.

'Look, Dad, I don't know. I just don't want to get married so I ain't goin' to, okay!'

'What? You giving me bloody orders, you stupid . . . I can't believe what the hell I'm hearing. Listen, Naila! You will go to your wedding even if I have to drag you there, you understand?' Naila's dad gave the final orders. Naila burst into tears and ran upstairs crying out, 'Dad, you not fair. I am not going.'

'You damn well are!' Naila's dad shouted while she ran upstairs. He threw the wooden leg on the floor with fury and shook his head.

Three hours later, Naila's mum and dad walked into Naila's room, before knocking of course. Naila was sitting on her bed, miserable. The tension had calmed down and her parents looked like they weren't sure what to expect. Naila turned away from her parents and coughed. Her mother had bought up some food and put it beside her. Naila turned around and looked at the food then glanced at her mother with love.

'Naila, I don't know what the hell is going on, but I want you to tell me everything,' Naila's dad said while shutting the door behind him.

CHAPTER 8

'I NEED TO see her, man. It's bugging me, bro. Have you got the yard number?' I impatiently spoke on the phone to Majid. It was twelve in the night, a week after Naila met up with Uncle Tarik. I know that because Uncle Tarik's family just left an hour ago and told us. It's a sign. I got to see her.

'Oh, yeah, give it to me. I'll ring her right now . . . I don't care, *mai,* let her dad pick it up. 0121, yeah, yeah, yeah, uh ha, uh ha, safe. Then bro, I'll ding you back in a bit to tell you wah-gwan,' I said while jotting a number down, then I ended the call.

I looked at the piece of paper I had written the number down on, then took a deep breath and dialled but didn't press *call* just yet.

At Naila's house, the house was quiet due to everyone being asleep besides Naila. She was sitting on her bed looking frustrated. She was thinking, *Why can't I sleep? Why is that idiot Shakiel messing with my heart now? I'm getting married soon. My dad knows something even though I told him there's nothing bugging me. I can't tell the truth because I don't even know what the hell is going on myself. Please, God, give me a break, give me some ease, give me a sign to let me know if I'm doing the right thing or not.* Naila's thoughts rushed out. Her throat and lips became dry so she got up for a drink.

The house was really dark. As she opened her door to leave, a wire got caught on Naila's ankle. 'What the hell is this?' Naila pulled her leg to free it from the wire but accidentally dropped something on the floor. *Ppprrrii!* 'Hello? Who's speaking? Hello?' The phone rang and was answered as the phone dropped to the floor.

'Oh, crap, it's the phone,' Naila said. She picked it up and took it to her room as she got her breath back. The person on the other line was still trying to talk.

Naila whispered as I chatted normally.

'Hello, can I ask who's speaking?' Naila asked. *Oh, my gosh! Her voice. The beautiful sound of her voice.*

'Er, is this Naila?' I replied. I was sweating and shivering but I really wanted to do it.

'Yeah, is this, err, who's this, is it . . .'

'It's me, Shakiel.'

Naila dropped the phone in shock.

Naila looked up to the sky out her window, thinking, *Not this soon.* She said, 'What do you want? You wanna speak to ma dad or, er, mum?'

'Well, I want to speak to you.' I smiled as Naila's heart started pounding. 'Listen, I know it's the wrong time, I mean, there's no right time for what I'm gonna say. You can stay quiet, but I need for you to know. Okay, here goes . . .'

I paused for about ten seconds. 'I realise you getting married and all. I'm happy for ya, but I gotta get this of ma chest. Since I been a kid, like you been ma childhood sweetheart. I know it sounds a bit cheesy, but I haven't really found an interest in other girls. Dunno why. Every time I see ya, you glowing, you outshine from the other. Jus now when I heard your voice, it was like the angels are talking to me. I mean, I gotta big-time crush on ya. I don't even know why I've rang you now, but I jus wanted you to know 'cuz it would have killed me inside to see you marry another guy without knowing if I had a shot or not. Damn, I scared ya, I'm sorry, Naila.'

Before the phone call, I had no idea of what the hell I was going to say. It just come out the way it come out.

Naila did not say anything for about a minute. I started thinking the worst, but then she said, 'I don't know what to say. You not messing about or nufin 'cuz this is sum serious sh . . .'

'Sorry, but na, I ain't blagging. I like you,' I interrupted her sentence.

Naila sat on her bed gobsmacked and then said in amazement, 'I . . . I . . . I want you to come here. I need to see you. Come to me.'

I put my fist to the air, thinking, *Gwan, Shak!* 'When shall I come? Wait there, what you saying, you want to see me?' I thought I celebrated too early.

She said, 'Have you been having strange things telling you to come to me? I mean signs. Do you think it's kismet because, don't tell anyone, I think I feel the same way about you.'

I put both fists to the air and also gave a silent roar, as if my team had just scored a goal.

'For years I wanted you to know,' we both said at the same time.

'Sorry,' Naila apologised.

'Don't worry,' I responded.

'It's been so obvious that you the one, but I couldn't say anything 'cuz of ma wedding and that, but aren't you getting married too?' Naila asked.

I thought for a bit, forgetting about my future plans. 'Oh, Shazin, na na, that's just rumours. I'll tell you the truth now, swear down. She wants me to marry her, but I don't see me with her. I don't even like her. I don't give a damn. I wanna marry you. I want you to be ma wifey. You the girl I want and always will be, even when I heard 'bout you getting married to ma 'cuz Ali. I don't know why, but I knew there was something about you, that I couldn't let it be. I knew 'bout your wedding for time now but I don't know why I . . .'

'Shut up and jus come here.' She laughed.

So this is how it feels to like someone you really like. Sweet.

She looked at her clock in her room. 'Oh, crap, it's late. I didn't realise the time. Hold on, Shak. Can I call you that? Anyway, meet me somewhere tomorrow, err, where we met first, okay, at noon. Okay. Okay, bye,' Naila said while being so high in the sky then coming back to earth after realising the time.

'Okay, you don't really like Ali, isn't it? If you don't, I'm gonna stop this wedding, even if your dad kills me, if you don't like Ali . . . Sweet, then that's a bonus. Sweet dreams. I ain't sleeping tonight.'

I put the phone down. Naila whispered as she put down the phone too, 'Same here, Shak.'

I never use the word *sweet*. I cannot believe I just done that. 'Shak, you bad boy,' I said to myself while falling on my bed backwards.

Eleven o'clock, I was already dressed to impress her. I couldn't believe that I was really meeting her today. It's like our first official date.

I went to town an hour early just in case, and because I was so excited. I kept on going to the men's room in HMV to see if I still looked as slick as I did before. People started to notice that I was always popping in and out the gents' room, but I didn't care.

Naila also went an hour earlier and was doing exactly the same thing as me: going in and out the ladies' toilets at HMV to see if she still looked as good as before. It was funny because we didn't see each other at all, and both toilets were right next to each other.

The cashier at HMV noticed something was going on: two smartly dressed Muslims looking excited about something and frequently visiting the toilets.

It was about five minutes to twelve and we both rushed out the toilets together whilst bumping into each other. 'Sorry,' I said, but I still didn't notice her as we both looked past each other to look for each other.

I walked out of the shopping centre and waited by the spot I had seen her last at. Naila stopped. She saw me looking for her but didn't go say or do anything. Naila thought deeply, *What am I doing? I'm going to be married soon and here I am trying to ruin what I already got. But I've been looking for this since the dream.*

I looked down disappointed, thinking, *She didn't turn up. It was just a lousy dream I had last night.* I pulled out my phone and rang Majid. It rang. Naila walked towards me slowly. I wanted to ring Majid to tell him, she didn't come. It was ringing. Naila came closer. I felt a presence of someone behind me, someone special. I put my head up and saw her coming to me; I lowered the phone as it was still ringing.

'Hey, Shakiel, how you doing? You all right?' Naila's voice made me gobsmacked. I could not speak a word. I was lost and daydreaming in her eyes, so beautiful.

'Shakiel, are you all right? You look lost. Shakiel, don't mess about.' Naila spoke, but I didn't hear a thing until, 'Shak! Why the hell you call me for? I'm bloody sleeping, you muppet!' Majid had answered the phone.

'Huh, oh, sorry.' I looked at my phone and cancelled the call.

'Naila, I swear, you look so fly today. I could've sworn you just threw away your halo somewhere, 'cuz you look so much like an angel.' I was stunned at the way her appearance was.

Naila laughed and looked at me. 'You looking pretty good yourself.'

We went to eat at McDonald's. We both ordered the same, obviously. The only good and *halal* thing at McDonald's is the fish burger.

We both sat opposite each other, waiting for the waiter to bring it to us. We didn't speak for a bit. I looked downwards while Naila looked right at me.

'I wanna be with you, but it's messed up for me, you know. I got it bad,' Naila said whilst also looking down.

'Naila, all I wanna do is be with you and satisfy you. I want you to be happy,' I replied.

'So, what did you say about going out today?' I asked while putting my hands on the table to fidget with the menu.

Naila looked at my hands and slowly put her hands on top of them. 'I told my mum that I'm visiting a college mate. But forget that. What we gonna do? You like me or what? 'Cuz if you don't, I won't be happy.'

'Na, it's not like that, we both jabooked. I know and I do like ya. You been on ma mind since I been a kid, man.'

I flipped my hands over so my palms were touching her palms. So soft. I felt a bit more relaxed. I was in another world just being next to her and feeling her touch.

The waiter came with the food and separated us by putting the tray of food between us.

'Thank you,' I said to the waiter. I looked over Naila's shoulder and said, 'Oh, shhh . . .'

'What, Shak?' Naila asked.

'It's bloody Zara. She's with her mates,' I whispered.

'Don't worry, she's cool. She's aite. She won't say nufin,' Naila said while turning around to look.

'Well, congratulations to Zara then. She'll be the first to know.' Naila took a bite out her burger.

I started stressing because we were going to be caught together. I ate my burger and fries quickly and went to the men's room, trying not to be noticed.

When I came back, Naila was chatting to Zara who had joined her on our table. I don't know what the hell Naila had told her while I was in the toilets, so I didn't know what to say when Zara suspiciously asked me, 'So, Shakiel, when's the big day?'

I started sweating because I wasn't sure who she was on about. If she was on about Naila, we hadn't even planned to get married, but if she was on about Shazin, then next year or in a few months; I didn't know. I didn't even care.

'She's asking when you gonna get married, Shak.' Naila really helped me there, *didn't she*?

'Err, next year, whenever you wanna get married, Naila.' I responded looking directly into the eyes of Naila.

Zara had a shocked expression, which Naila had noticed.

'Na, really Shakiel, stop messing around. With Shazin.' Naila shook her head behind Zara.

'Sorry, I'm only messin. Yeah in about six to twelve months time. We haven't arranged a set date yet. Anyway, what's happenin wiv you these days?' I tried to change the subject.

'Nothing much. Going uni, that's all,' Zara replied while eating some fries from the tray.

Zara was a person you could trust. She kept your things to herself as well as other people's issues, but I didn't want to take the risk and mess things up at this stage.

In fifteen minutes of talking to her, hesitating hesitated on all the questions she asked, even if they were like, 'How's your mum?' Zara knew something was going on, but she didn't say anything about us being together.

Zara and her friends left, and both of us said that, 'That was close.'

We strolled around in town just talking for about an hour and a half. 'It's strange. Yesterday about this time, I didn't ever think it would be you and me. I mean, yesterday you were just a boy to me, but now you my boy. Do you think anyone will understand us being together?' Naila said while holding my hand.

'Besides your mum, you know when she told you my name in the car and that, besides your mum, everyone's gonna gun me down. My mum's gonna go, 'You bloody going out wiv a gal that's bloody getting married in two months?' then probably slap me or something.'

We both laughed. I never wanted the day to end, but Naila wanted to go home before she got deeper in her father's bad book. We both had different buses to catch so I waited by Naila for her bus to come first.

'You know I'm older than you, Shak. It ain't a problem, is it? A *whole* two years.' Naila looked at me like I was going to walk away or something.

'Of course it's a bloody problem. I'm gonna have to find myself a Naila who's exactly like you but my age.' I giggled, and a second later Naila giggled.

'Hold on, before you go, let me take a picture of you because all this time I've . . . I know it's cheesy, but I've kept a picture of you for time now in ma wallet.'

I pulled out ma phone and took a picture of her. I took a few actually and told her the others were not coming out right. I then pulled out my wallet and took out the picture I had of her.

'Whoa, that picture's old. Where did you get it from? Whoa, you do have a big-time crush on me. I wish you had told me sooner. Look, if we never get together, here's a little present from me to you.' Naila gave me the picture back and, as I put it back in my wallet, she leaned over and kissed me on my lips. My eyes opened fully as I saw her on me and was surprised at first but then enjoyed it. Hold on, let me finish. I wish that kiss would never end.

I looked around to see if anyone saw. 'Yo, you crazy or something? We ain't allowed to kiss, but thanks anyways for that present.'

'It's aite. You needed it. You got a piece of me now, even if I don't marry you, and why can't we kiss?' Naila questioned while getting on the bus.

'We can kiss only if you really *really* love the other person and the other person loves you and has intentions to get married. And a husband is allowed to kiss a wife and a child is allowed to kiss their parents and vice versa.' I rambled on explaining while Naila smiled and raised one eyebrow.

Naila waved me goodbye.

I was still dazed after the kiss; I was in another world until someone nudged me to go onto the bus.

'Sorry, this ain't my bus,' I apologised.

I started walking towards my bus stop, thinking, *Naila loves me. Do I love her? I have no idea. I probably do but don't even know it. Of course I do. I've had a crush on her since I was a kid. I can't believe what just took place.*

I waited for the bus for a few minutes then jumped on when it came. I was still astonished after the kiss. Subhanallah.

CHAPTER 9

'I FEEL ON top of the world, man,' I told Majid on the phone while looking at the picture of her on my phone. 'I had the best time with her . . . She made me feel things inside for her like, you know . . . Yeah, hold on.' I lowered the phone as I heard shouting coming from downstairs.

'Cousin, I gorra go, safe.' I put the phone down then opened my drawer and took out my homemade knuckle-duster. It was a leather glove with iron studs super-glued to the sides, front and back (not on the palm). I wore it because my mum's cousin's brother, Rafik kept on telling my mum off for everything that was going wrong in her life. I couldn't do anything about it before because I was too young, too afraid, and my mum and dad told me to respect my elders while growing up. I am not a kid anymore more, and no one's going to push my mum around now because I'm going to deal with it. This will be the last time Uncle Rafik is going to come over to visit.

My mum was crying when I came down. I stayed by the top of the staircase out of view from them. I stepped down a few steps, but Uncle Rafik still couldn't see me as he was shouting at my mum, 'You wanna be a loser, go be one. I don't give a damn, but look after your kids properly. I mean, your boy's a druggy. Where the hell do you think he gets his money from, the government? He ain't getting any money from them. They ain't gonna give that prick any money. Look at him. He's meant to be at uni now. He needs some butt whipping to put him into shape. I mean, he ain't even got a driving licence and he's been driving illegally for two or three years.'

Uncle Tarik kissed his teeth and then continued. 'Your girl, Tara, what the hell's going on with her? She doesn't have any manners at all. I've been here for an hour now and she hasn't even offered me anything to drink or eat. I know you will now but you only going to be doing it because I've said it. Bloody waste of time and space, you are,' Uncle Rafik said while pointing and forcing his finger into my mum's shoulder.

Tara quickly went to get a drink ready from the fridge. She was overhearing in the dining room.

'Yo, Raf, my dad's been passed away time back now. When was the last time, I mean first time, I mean *ever*—whenever have you helped out with things when we have needed help?' I said with confidence while still sitting down on the staircase. 'We've needed help financially, mentally, physically, and the worst thing is you knew we needed help but you didn't do jack, did you?'

'Shakiel, go up. You don't need to hear this!' my mum cried out.

'Oh, so your son thinks he's all that, he thinks he can talk rude to me? Your whole family's lost the plot. You are all idiots, you know? No family will want their daughter or son in this household because they will just be calling their mother—and father-in-laws by their flipping nicknames. I'm your uncle, you prick, calling me Raf!'

'Yo, I don't care if you were Shah Rukh Kahn, speaking 'bout ma mum like that you just asking to get beats, mai.'

I came down slowly with my lethal hand in my pocket. Tara entered the lounge with a drink for Uncle Rafik.

'Tara, give me that.' Uncle Rafik snatched the cold drink out of Tara's hand and spilt most of it on himself and the floor. He shouted, 'Look what you done now, you stupid imbecile.'

'Rafoo, don't call my daughter names,' my mum struggled to say, while Uncle Rafik tried cleaning his top with his handkerchief. Then he laughed at my mum, saying, 'Did I hear you correctly, lil 'cuz? Did I hear correctly, the one who used to cry when I used to beat the crap out her brother? Did I hear correctly? You could not do anything then and you cannot do anything now. When your bro used to cry, I felt sorry for you. I said to myself, 'Who the hell is she gonna go to when she needs someone to back her case? Her parents are dead. I ain't gonna do crap for her. Her brother's a wussy.' Uncle Rafik laughed. 'This drink's gone warm. Go put it in the fridge, Tara, and clean this up. Someone's gonna come any minute now and see this place is a tip.' Uncle Rafik pointed to the floor where he had spilt his drink.

'Tara, you drink the drink,' I said. 'Listen, you joke, you've messed around with my family too many times, so I'm saying get out ma yard or let ma fist say hello to your face.'

Uncle Rafik turned from me to look at my mum. 'Look what your son's saying. He definitely has lost the plot. I'm gonna have to beat some sense into him, just like I beat your flipping brother.'

My mum screamed out, 'Don't hurt him! He's just a kid! Hit me, hit me, beat on me, please don't hurt Shakiel!' My mum burst into more tears.

Uncle Rafik looked at my mum and walked slowly towards me, then *boof!* Uncle Rafik backslapped my face. I stepped back nearly falling, still with my hand in my pocket. My mum and Tara screamed as he slapped me.

'Don't hurt my son anymore! Hit me if you wanna get your anger out. He's just a kid, Rafoo. Who are you proving you a big man to?' My mum grabbed Uncle Rafik's shoulder from behind as he was still looking at me while I was getting back to conscious.

Uncle Rafik turned around and clenched his fist with fury. 'My pleasure,' he said as he went to attack my mum.

I took my hand out of my pocket and turned him around. 'Hello.' *Bang!* Got him.

Uncle Rafik dropped on the floor with six stud marks bleeding out of his left cheek.

My mum and Tara screamed again but immediately started cheering. My mum looked like she won the lottery or something; she looked like she felt a sense of relief.

I felt good too, helping my mum and all, but also felt gutted. Uncle Rafik is married to Naila's dad's cousin's sister and he is also my mum's dad's brother's son. So, getting with Naila is probably out of the equation even more now, but I would do anything for my mum. Uncle Rafik got up in the centre of the lounge with my mum, Tara and myself surrounding him. I had given my mum my baseball bat, I had given Tara my dumbbell poles, and I still had my knuckle-duster.

'He's awake, Mum. Give my man here what he deserves,' I said as my mum swung the bat on his back, saying, 'You do not come in my house telling me how to live it. It's my house, it's my life and my kids. Oh, and that there was from my brother. Tara, give your uncle some nice and cold ice with his drink,' my mum told Tara as Uncle Tarik had fallen down again after my mum had hit him. Tara waited for the right moment. Uncle Rafik struggled to get on his knees. He was a total mess but Tara did not care. She swung both the poles and sandwiched it to the side of his head. *Smack!*

I helped him up to his knees and knelt down in front of him. 'Yo, Raf, you still here? Listen, yeah, your time has passed, man, so I ain't gonna hit you anymore, but you gonna have to get the hell outta ma yard before I change my mind. I don't want you ever stepping foot in this house again, and I'll make sure of that, you understand mai?' I put my fist in front of his face.

Uncle Rafik nodded and got up with great effort then limped out the house.

My mum looked at me, saying, 'I've always wanted to do that. He used to beat your mamu up and your mamu always used to tell me after that he wishes our dad was here to knock him out. Your mamu used to hate him as a cousin. I hated him too. I still do. Thank you for that. At least I know me and ma bro got our payback. Did you see how I hit his back with the . . . the bat?'

I laughed. 'Yeah, I saw you. Listen, Mum, you gonna tell me if he still attempts to worry you. I'll do anything for you, you know, and you too, T,' I said as I looked at my mum and Tara.

'I lost my respect for him the day he came to our house and started on you for no reason. No, it wasn't for no reason, it was because he said you were the reason Dad's gone. Remember that day, Mum? He'll phone or come again to trouble you again, all you gotta do is put me on the phone or if he's here when I'm not, ring me. I'll come home from wherever I am and sort him out.'

My mum took off my glove and threw it on the floor.

Tara chucked the poles on the floor and said, 'I know it's not the right time, but are we going to get punished for hitting him and err disrespecting him, because if we are, I don't want to hit anyone again, especially someone who's gonna come back for us.'

'Don't worry, T, he has got to have a lot of nerve to come back here, but if he *does* comes back and he ain't planning to apologise for anything he's done or wants us to say sorry, well that's when I'll have to teach an old-schooler a few sum lessons.'

We heard Uncle Rafik drive off then we all laughed in joy.

About half an hour later, Naila phoned our house. Luckily, I answered it. Naila was in her room with Shamala.

'Hello . . . Yeah, hey Shakiel, I heard what happened. Yeah, news travels fast in our community. I know why you did it, I would do the same thing if my uncle came down my house and said stuff like that about my mum and dad. I would want something done about it if I couldn't handle it. I know he's my mamu or cousin mamu or whatever he is to me, but anyone can see he isn't a nice guy. I don't like how he speaks to people. He's so rude . . . Huh . . . Yeah, I realised. I know we are probably screwed to get together now, but no one knows about us and no one has to know for a while . . . What do you mean how I got your number? It's in our address book under your mum's name, duh. Anyway, Ali phoned me. He told me to send him some more emails with attached pictures of myself so he can show his mates . . . I ain't sending him jack, you know.'

She paused to catch her breath. 'Shak, between me and you . . . and Shamala, yeah, I told Shamala about us. It's all right; she figured it out anyway. Anyway, already it's like I'm his wife. I got to do all his dirty work while he lazes about chilling with his mates or sitting in watching movies and stuff. Shamala told me this isn't the life for me and that I don't like him . . . Na, I don't . . . I'm telling you the truth, Shakiel. I know I'm gonna be miserable with him. Last week, he made me chill with his mates, okay. His mates were driving fancy cars, you know, top of the range, but still I had to buy food, not only for Ali and me but his three bloody starving mates. And that's not all. Ali made me buy them about five rounds of snooker and change for the gambling machines. They took my money to use for gambling. *Astagfirullah* . . . I know . . . Shakiel, I made my mind up two days ago. I want to be with you. I had a great time with you. You treated me nicely. I want to be with you even if it causes havoc and chaos . . . No, I'm telling you . . . I'm telling you . . . No, listen . . . No, it's the truth . . . No listen, I'm telling you in plain English.'

Naila started crying, 'I wanna, I don't wanna be with someone like Ali. He, he, he uses me and when we married, he's gonna use me even more than before. His mum's already shouting at me for things I'm supposed to know. She makes me feel so low. His dad just looks mean at me in an evil way and makes me want to cry just looking at him, and that's when we visiting him with my parents. What do you think he's gonna do when no one's around? I don't want to go to that, so Shakiel, I want the marriage not to happen in the first place. Help me, please . . . No, I can't tell Ali. Please, Shak, you do something. He'll kill me and you . . . We have to run away or something . . . Huh, *allow that*. What does that mean? Okay. Why? Is she waiting for the phone? Okay, ring me on my mobile later. Tara's got ma number. Listen, we got to link up again, sort something out. Where shall we link . . . Okay, at four, no problem.

Shakiel, listen . . . I know that we've only been out once, but I miss you already . . . Oh, yeah, thank you . . . For the last time, when we went out, I liked it . . . Okay . . . salaams.'

Naila put the phone down and sighed. 'Shamala, I'm so dead,' Naila told Shamala before falling back on her bed.

My mum wanted to use the phone so I had to cut the conversation short. *Damn, news travels fast. I bet they know back home what happened. Uncle Rafik gets me so vexed; he got what he deserved for all those things he's done.* My mum was talking to Uncle Rafik's wife (double damn). She started apologising like hell then eventually started crying. Tara sat by her to try ease the anxiety by stroking her back and giving her tissue for her tears.

'Look what we caused, Shak. It all seemed fun and games when we had control, but at the end of the day Uncle Rafik runs the place. You know how he is. He *will* come back and give Mum double trouble.' Tara looked at our mother. I thought for a moment then took the phone from my mum. My mum tried getting it back because she knew I'd say something stupid, but I didn't let her get the phone.

'Salaam, you all right, Aunty? . . . No, it's not like that, I mean, it's because . . . Yeah, it's . . . I understand. Look, listen, you not listening . . . Okay, I don't know if you see it, but Uncle Rafik treats my mum like crap . . . Yeah, like dog crap. You don't have to sort him out, but he ain't ever coming in my house and treating my mum like crap again, and I know you know because everyone knows how he is. He was gonna beat my mum up. He's beaten her up before.

No one did anything about it. Did you? No . . . Yeah, he was gonna beat my mum up again, and only the Almighty knows how many times he's beaten her up before, but this time I stopped it. If it meant teaching him a lesson to stop him, well that's how it had to be. I know you would do the same if I was to come to your house and beat on your children. You wouldn't like it one bit. I would've probably gone out your drive in a ambulance knowing how vexed Uncle Rafik gets . . . As long as I'm alive, my mum or sis ain't getting touched by no man violently, and if they do, well I feel sorry for their parents or partners because they would have lost someone they love . . . Err, no you can't speak to my mum; she's already in a state because of you. Look, I think it's best if we don't speak for a while. Let the news die out because . . . No . . . Look, and another thing, all those times he's come here, my mum ends up crying every time he's left—probably hit her, sworn at her, said bad things to her, I don't know. I know he's beat her up . . . Yeah, and how come you never told the world about that? You the one who tells everyone everything. How come you forgot to mention that to everyone? And this you make it a big thing and blew it up for the whole community . . . I'm getting phone calls from my cousins telling me what the hell have you done? Me and my family have just been sitting here the whole time, not doing a thing. I don't picture Uncle Rafik phoning everyone and telling them what happened, so it can only be you . . . You just afraid to hear the truth . . . No, I ain't lying . . . Fine, erase my family from your phone book . . . No, I ain't gonna . . . Fine . . . Don't . . . She don't want to hear the stuff you want to tell her . . . I'm gonna put the phone down . . . Salaam . . . No . . . Ring again, and I'll put it out straight away . . . And I thought you erasing my number from your phone book . . . Yeah, go do that, yeah . . . Salaam.'

I finally put the phone down. I looked at my mum and sister who had a look on their faces to say, 'You're so stupid, but I wouldn't trade you for the world.'

Uncle Rafik's wife didn't phone again.

CHAPTER 10

MY FRIEND SAJID had just texted to give me the details for a small school reunion. I replied to the text with, 'safe.' It was the next day. I had a little lie in because I wanted to clear my mind a bit, plus I had a late night. I couldn't stop thinking about Naila last night. She phoned my house, just to speak to me. She wanted to go out with me again. I could not believe it. I got out of bed and walked to the bathroom with my eyes half open.

'Shakiel, if this ever happens again, I'm going to slap you with my *chumpal,*' my mother said from her room.

'What?' I asked, thinking it had to do with yesterday's incident.

'If you ever wake up this late again, you going to get it,' my mother replied.

I sighed in relief, also giggling, 'Okay, Mum, it won't happen again. Sorry.' I looked in the mirror, seeing my sleepy face. I thought for a moment then realised something. Oh, crap! I'm going to link those boys in a bit and also going out with Naila at four. How am I going to get both things done within . . . What time is it? I walked out of the bathroom and looked at the clock in the hallway. Half three. No wonder my mother is screwing at me. Damn.

I quickly showered and got ready. As I did, I thought of a plan. I got out of the house and jumped in my car while texting. I drove in speed thinking I was going to make a few people unhappy if I was late.

Quarter past four.

'Shakiel, bro, what's good in the hood?' Sajid greeted me at the door as I walked into the *sheesha* lounge where the small reunion was.

'Nothing much, bro. Where's the boys?' I enquired while shaking Sajid's hand.

'They inside. Yo, Shak, I've never met her. Who's this you bringing with you?' Sajid raised his eyebrow with inquisitive behaviour while looking at the person behind me.

'Chill, cousin, she's a mate of mine. I was linking her as well so thought I'd come with her too. Is that Okay, Saj?' I said while looking back at Naila.

Naila smiled.

'Yeah, the more, the better. Asim bought his girl along too, so minor. It's cool. Come in.' Sajid walked in with us. I had texted Naila to walk down her road so I could pick her up, then both of us came to this reunion. She agreed so here we are.

The lounge was so cloudy from all the smoke coming from the sheeshas. My schoolmates were all sitting in the front corner with five ordered sheeshas. I looked at Naila to say, 'We can go if you not comfortable,' but it didn't seem to bother her, which I thought was really cool.

They all greeted me as I introduced Naila as a friend. There were six people: Anwar, Arfan, Zohaib, Asim and his girl, and Sajid. As we both sat down, Naila whispered, 'Shakiel, are you going to get one? I don't do it so carry on if you want, but I do enjoy the smell of it. The scent is so sweet.'

'I'm more hungry so I'm gonna get us both some food first, then I'll probably get one,' I answered. I noticed the guys all looking at Naila in a keen manner. Naila gave of a God-fearing expression as she kept her gaze low, trying not to get anyone's attention. Eventually, they took their awareness away from her and started taking notice of each other.

'Shak, remember the days when we'd all just be chilling after school, enjoying a phat session behind Mr. Jackson's car, and that one time we got clocked,' Zohaib said while passing the sheesha to Anwar.

'Yeah, man, we got done. We all got suspended for four days, except Saj. He goes he wasn't with us even though he clearly was. Jackson couldn't tell how many boys were there. Not surprised he missed ya, Saj.' I laughed.

Sajid sniggered, 'Yeah, if I got done, my mum would've kicked ma ass man, trust me. Times were hard, man.'

I couldn't believe Naila was sitting next to me, I couldn't believe she was with us at the sheesha lounge, just chilling with us. I wanted to tell the world that she was my dream girl. My childhood sweetheart. But I couldn't. It was too complicated. Every few minutes, I'd just glimpse at her and smile. She was actually enjoying herself. She spoke with Asim's girl for the majority of the time, but I didn't mind.

After ten minutes, our food came.

'Is there a special guy in your life at the moment, Naila?' Zohaib grinned. I wish I could tell them to lay off, but I had told them she was just a friend.

'Well, I am set to get married soon, so I guess the answer is yes,' she retorted. 'I wish I wasn't so good sometimes, like I listen to my parents too much. They've like sorted me out with this one guy and I've listened and agreed just to please them. Only now, when there's little or no time left, I've realised that I don't want to do what they want anymore. I want to do what I want. I want to choose who I want, knowing them. If God wills I have children, they going to name it and raise it how they want. I know I have to put my foot down some time, but I'm such a little softy when I'm in front of them.' Naila picked up her glass of juice.

'Preach!' exclaimed Asim's girl.

Asim looked at her with cross-eye brows. 'Are you saying you don't wanna be with me? Allow you then,' Asim jokingly said.

Asim's girl put her head down in shame but raised it again while laughing.

Time passed. We both had eaten and I had to go the gents' room to freshen up. Naila had also gone to do the same thing. I went into the gent's room, washed my hands and face, and then looked in the mirror. *This is too good to be true. The girl I've always wanted is right in the next room.* The biggest grin came on my face.

Naila washed her face then started doing her hair. She put her makeup bag on the sink table and pulled her lipstick out. She pasted her lips with a glossy maroon then kissed her lips. She looked in the mirror and shrugged as if to say she was satisfied of how she looked. She then looked closer. Her lips were twitching. She then went in deep and thought, *I can't believe I'm here with Shakiel. He's so cool. I want to be with him always, I swear. If he doesn't sort something out for both of us, I'm going to shoot him, even if I really like him.* The twitching turned into a wide grin. Naila even started chuckling. She finished up and then walked out of the girls' room where she noticed me walking towards the crowd again. 'Shakiel!' Naila shouted out.

I turned around and saw her, my heart pounding harder than ever. I walked towards her in such a rush and said, 'You all right, Naila? What's wrong?'

'Nothing, sorry, I don't know why I just done that. Well, I just want to be with you. Now that you here, can I see you for a moment, in the corner there?' Naila pointed to the empty far corner.

We both walked and sat down in the corner; she placed her hand on my knee. 'Shak, I'm really enjoying our time together. I really like your friends. They sound on a level, erasing out all the nonsense you guys did in school, but yeah, they really cool, especially you, thanks for bringing me.'

'It's nothing. I really enjoy spending time with you too, like the first time we went out was like I was dreaming, and this time, I really can't believe you here with me right now. Swear down, I'm feeling contentment,' I replied while getting excited.

Naila got closer and said, 'Shakiel, please do something so I don't get married soon, that I get the best guy and not the guy I'm going to be forced with. You know when we just came and you introduced me to your friends, I felt like a wife. Being part of your life would mean the world to me. Like you said, I also feel contentment in my heart, and I feel so safe around you.'

'I'll try, but you know this as much as I do. This is going to be like starting a world war there after making world peace, plain difficult,' I answered. I noticed she had done her makeup again. Her face was so shiny, especially her lips. I wanted her to kiss me again. I wanted another picture of her. I wanted this moment never to end. I *wanted* her.

'Shakiel, let's go back. They gonna think things about us.' She stood up.

'Okay, Naila,' I agreed.

We sat back down with Sajid and the others. After fifteen minutes, Anwar and Arfan greeted us as they both got up and left. The rest of us decided to go together after a further twenty minutes.

'You still on the deen scene, Shak?' Sajid asked.

'Kinda. I pray as much as I can. Sometimes I get all five in, but there's other times I only manage like three or four. It's really changed my life though, like I don't mess about anymore. I'm controlling the *nafs* more than before, so think it ain't so bad. What about you, Saj?' I said while smiling at Naila as if to say she's the one who's changed my life for the better.

'Yeah, man, always am, always will, not saying I'm big and that, but I completed my forty days after we finished school, went for *hajj* during first year of college and got intentions to go do my four months after uni, haven't missed a day of salah, man. It's too important. It's a command that was given in heaven to the most Beloved as a gift. The Miraj is a beautiful story, subhanallah. You know, if your salah is correct, your day will be correct, your life will be correct, your afterlife will be right and sorted.

'Check this, cousin. We should box it off in this life so we boxed off in the hereafter. It's the answer to all problems, but no one sees it. You want help with anything, the main man's waiting for you and salah is your direct connection with Him. Listen, I ain't lecturing you guys, you know me, I'm just telling you the truth. I was on those vibes once, *remember*, shotting, juggling, living the thug life, but it don't do feck-all for ya, bro, besides really messing your life up. Only thing I do that's frowned upon is this, sheesha, but I see it as a means of getting together with the youth so I can spread this message to them. Oh, it's also a really good medicine, clears out all the sinuses. But yeah, don't put anything in-between you and the Almighty. You only ask from Him, people think man-made things will help them in this life. For example, Shak, you get a headache, you go have a painkiller, that's already putting something before you and the Almighty. You thinking the paracetamol will clear your head? No, cousin, it's the Almighty who clears it. You go towards the Almighty first, then take the paracetamol as a means of cure given by the Almighty.

'Listen I'm telling you this because something happened to my cousin a while back. You remember my cousin, Dawood. In year nine, when we were in year eleven, yeah, well, he was cruising with his *bedrin* in a rental, the Almighty decided to take his life along with his bedrins, sixteen now, and he's in his grave with how many right and good deeds and intentions. You know that geeza was a chiller on the streets: girls, drugs, you name it. Only the Lord knows how he was, but yeah, life is too short to be messing around. This is the time to make a change to ourselves, so when we go from this world, we go in the Lord's good books, you get me? We gorra chill with people who will benefit us in the hereafter, not bedrins that will put you in the grave with regret. You know where to be, where the angels are, the masjid? That's where we should go chill, chill with the angels. They'll benefit us.' Sajid put the rest of us in astonishment.

'Yeah, man, will try to,' I gulped.

'Yo, Shak, I'm still feeling that hit from town that time. You one dangerous guy. I gorra start chilling with you again, will benefit by having a hard knock around,' Sajid elucidated.

I laughed and apologised at the same time by putting my hand over his shoulder. We all chipped in and paid the bill then left the sheesha lounge, greeting each other as we all went in our separate ways.

I went to drop Naila off. I had to park a road away from her house, just in case someone saw us.

'Okay, see you, Naila. Soz about Saj and his lecturing; I swear he never used to be like that in school,' I said while parking up.

'No way, he's cool. He *does* speak so much sense, really gets you thinking. Anyways, see you. I'll call you later.'

Naila jumped out of the car.

'I forgot to give you something,' Naila said while surprising me. Just before closing the door she looked in and blew me a kiss. For some reason, I felt it hit my cheek.

'Asalaamu Alaikum, Shakiel. Drive safe.' She shut the door and walked towards her road.

I was over the moon. Naila was actually with me. Naila just blew me a kiss. Naila was sitting in my car, right next to me. Naila actually wants to be with me. Wow.

Subhanallah.

CHAPTER 11

IT WAS THREE weeks till Naila's and Ali's wedding day. I had gone out with Naila two more times after the reunion, and both times I didn't want to say bye to her. I still thought I was dreaming. I couldn't wait to see her again and again. It was getting serious, to a point where both of us liked each other so much we were ready to tell everyone to their faces, but when it came to telling people we automatically got cold feet.

Shamala, Majid, and Tara were the only ones who knew. Tara found out because Naila phoned her a few times and asked for me when I didn't answer my own phone and got a bit suspicious. A few days ago, Tara asked me if I were seeing her in secret, and when I said no, she could tell I was lying. She said, 'I know you are, so stop lying.' So I said, 'Aite, we are, but don't tell anyone, okay?'

Anyway, talk about dilemma. I was in Ali's room, helping out with the decoration for the wedding, with Ali and his dad. It was quite late in the afternoon when I thought, *Shall I tell him or not?* Naila told me she would tell him in good time and if I told then he would break my legs and give them back to me. So I thought twice and didn't tell him. I was still on a level with Ali. We weren't talking eye to eye but we were talking.

'So Shak, you a hard knock these days. You beat up on family that are elder than you. You wanna beat me up?' Ali's dad giggled out while gently jabbing my arm.

'Huh, na, na, just family that mess about, mess around with my mum. My mum doesn't have anyone to protect her and seeing as I'm her son, I thought it's my responsibility, ineh,' I replied as Ali looked at me surprisingly.

Ali put tinsel over the bed, making a shape of a heart, then said, 'Naila's gonna love it here. She already does. Last week she goes that she wants to have some alone time, just her in the room. I left her, and after about ten minutes I walk in and she is sleeping so peacefully, on her side of the bed. I woke her up to watch a film with me so we watched it. Then she had to go home—her dad started calling her.' I looked at the heart that he had put up and asked, 'Do you love her, bro?'

'Love is for losers, love is for pricks like my dad had been, when he had no time for his boys and that. I'd rather not go down that route. I'd love to be like ma dad now, though, an OG in the hood. I mean, everyone knows me in this area 'cuz of ma pops, man. He's a big timer, you get me? I also love to take control, just how ma dad does over ma mum. I see it as if you love someone, you both are equal and gotta share responsibilities. I rather give her all the responsibilities while I chilax, inneh, Dad?' Ali explained as he nodded to his dad

His dad added, 'The whole idea is that you put fear in her. If she fears you, you'll get results; trust me on that one.' Ali's dad was sweeping up the mess then put the broom down, wiped sweat of his forehead, and took out a ready-to-smoke sheesha from underneath the cupboard table. He puffed on it and passed it to Ali.

Ali's dad walked out the room and went downstairs. Ali said while smoking the sheesha, 'Yeah, now that ma dad's gone, Naila's gonna make ma life so much fun and easy as well as doing everything. I'm gonna be loving it in bed, you get me?'

Ali passed the pipe and I responded by saying, 'Do what you want, but treat her right, yeah? I would.' I exhaled the smoke with a cheeky smile.

'*Who* would treat *her* right? What the hell, man, look at her. She's made to please.' Ali took the pipe and started smoking it violently.

'I was just saying that good girls like Naila will leave you if you don't treat them right,' I clarified. I tried putting some sense into his head about not to abuse Naila, but Ali countered back, 'Yeah, right, man, if she even thinks of running away, I'll bloody handcuff her to ma bed, then she'll learn she can't run from me. She can stay there for good.' Ali laughed. 'Make her ass stay by the bed.'

Ali continued to laugh as I kept a straight face. Ali noticed me not laughing and said, 'What?'

Before I could say anything, my phone rang. I saw the caller ID. It was Rizwan. I walked out and answered it. He told me if I was broke, if I wanted to make so much money, I wouldn't need to work again if I would do this last mission with him. I'm a sucker when it comes to money, so I agreed. Rizwan also told me to link him up in town at the usual spot, in an hour's time, and to wear dark clothes. He added that three other boys would be doing it with us this time. We both knew and could trust two of them. I knew the third guy, but—I don't know why—I can't trust someone who's not Asian.

'I have to go link ma mate up bro, it's an emergency. I'll catch you later, yeah,' I told Ali as I waved him goodbye.

I walked down and said salaams to my uncle and aunty who were talking in the kitchen. I then walked out the house.

Three million pounds split between five people, I couldn't stop thinking about it as I drove home to get changed.

Iyaz and Malik were the two guys we could trust. They both worked for the same delivery service, which exported cocaine to the Big Boss of the Mid-West. The exports were hidden in pencil case boxes and the Big Boss sold then in hundreds. Iyaz and Malik were not meant to know what they were delivering, but they overheard the Big Boss telling the supplier that it was his payday and gangs from all over the Mid-West were going to buy it all and the worth of all the cocaine sold would be eight million pounds, but the Big Boss would transfer five million pounds to his bank account and blow three million pounds cash on whatever the hell he wanted. Our plan was to somehow knock him out when everyone was gone, even when his own boys were gone. Our fifth boy Jason, a white boy, was going to be the lookout.

'There's the Italian mafia, man,' Malik pointed out to a gang that was walking into the porter cabin while we all hid behind a garage shutter of an old car company.

'You got your gat, Shak? This might go down a bit ugly, you get me?' Rizwan told me.

'I don't leave it behind in situations like this, mai. You should know this, bro.' I patted on my back pocket where I kept my special nine-millimetre gun. I got two guns of this dealer a few years back. He ripped me off on one as it was only a BB gun, and the other one was a genuine nine-millimetre.

'Hey, why didn't you guys just take the coke and sell it yourselves?' asked Jason.

'I don't like to get involved in drugs, man, but I do like money you get from it, baby,' replied Iyaz.

We waited patiently for half an hour. It was dark and getting pretty cold in the garage, but luckily everyone, including the Big Boss's boys, had left.

Jason went across the road to keep a lookout. Four of us put our scarves and hoods up and walked towards the cabin where the Big Boss was.

'Take a deep breath, boys. This is gonna get ugly,' I said while inhaling before going into the cabin. Iyaz kicked open the door.

'Freeze, this is a holdup so hold your hands up, nigga!' Malik shouted as we all walked in and closed the door. I walked towards the Big Boss who was stunned; before we walked in, he was counting his money. *Bang!* I punched him across his face with my knuckle-duster. He fell off his chair and onto the floor. He was out cold by the look of him.

'Put the money in the bags that he's got here, quick,' I said while looking on his computer. They all rushed putting the money in bags that the Big Boss was going to use for the money anyway. I noticed something. I felt butterflies, but not the kind when I'm around Naila—a whole different category of butterflies. I called Rizwan over. 'He hasn't sent the money to his account yet. You thinking what I'm thinking, bro? Between me and you, we deserve it.'

I looked at the other two and saw that they were still putting the money in the bags. I pulled out my wallet and took out my debit card. I got the keyboard and entered my account details in and clicked on '*Send transfer.*' We both gave the craziest grin ever.

'You punk ass, this is firstly for calling me a nigger!' the Big Boss coughed out as he pulled a gun from under his desk and fired it at Malik; at the same time the computer screen blinked out, 'Transfer completed.'

Bang!

Malik dropped to the ground as all of us screamed out, 'Nooo!'

'And this is for knocking me out and pissing me off!' the Big Boss got up slowly then aimed the gun at me. I took cover behind the desk and took out my gun. The other three hid behind cabinets and chairs that were stacked up. Rizwan crawled to where I was then pointed to tell me where the Big Boss was so I could get him with a clear shot.

'Forget this, man, not over yeyo. My man's going down, frigging shooting Malik and dat. No way he's getting away with dat. Listen, Riz, I know I'm gonna be going to hell for this, but, *Aahhhh!*' I fired several shots towards the Big Boss as I got up.

Blood rushed out of the Big Boss's arm and chest. The Big Boss had a tense look on his face until he gave up and let the pain get the better of him.

I shot him. I killed him. I killed him. I killed a man. I killed the Big Boss.

What the hell have I done? What the hell am I doing here? Oh, no, my mum, my sister, Naila. I've done wrong to them. Everyone was in silence for about two minutes until sirens went off.

'We got to get out of here, guys!' Jason said as he poked his head through the door. 'What the hell happened in here? Listen, I don't wanna know. We got to go. It's popo.'

We ran out as fast as we could, which wasn't that fast as we were holding Malik and the bags of money. They were heavy and also bloody.

Police got into the cabin as we just reached our car. The police found the Big Boss dead, but they also found another person's blood on the floor. Damn.

We had to think, and we had to think fast. We were driving off quite fast and it looked so obvious, but we were so ahead of them that the police wouldn't catch us up even if they wanted to chase us.

Jason was driving. Iyaz was in the passenger seat and Malik, Rizwan, and I were in the back. Malik was lying across both of us. I said to myself while looking at Malik, 'Was it worth it, getting this money for one of ma homeys to get shot? What the hell have we done? Why didn't I think before I agreed to this?'

Malik was still breathing but struggling with a lot of pain. Malik agonisingly spoke out his last words: 'Don't tell my mum, please, don't tell my . . .'

Tears poured out our eyes. Three million pounds for four people now. Why am I not chuffed?

CHAPTER 12

A WEEK HAD passed since the big robbery, not a penny spent, and we had to break the news to Malik's parents. We all had to have a straight story and stick with it, no matter what we had to go through. The story was that we were all walking down this road and a car drove past, shot at us for no reason, and shot Malik. If we told the truth, we would have all gone to jail. We had to hide the money until all the trouble cleared up.

Malik was a big timer, so his family told us that he had it coming sooner or later. What a thing to say about their son!

Malik's funeral was done within three days after his death. We all cried as we lost another brother.

We all thought we dodged a big bullet by not getting caught, but I spoke too soon. It took a whole week for the police to identify my fingerprints on the bullet that shot the Big Boss. I was on my computer in my room on MSN messenger, chatting to Majid about Naila and also about what had happened in a code language to prevent any suspicion on us. *Bang!* A big boot to my door and it broke from the hinges and fell to the floor.

'Are you Shakiel? You are under arrest for the murder of Jeff Maxwell, who was also known as the Big Boss. There will be no court hearing due to clear evidence that you were the killer. Anything you say will . . .'

A police officer reported me then I interrupted. 'Hold on. Firstly, ma door was flippin' open. Secondly, I don't know what the heck you on about. I closed my conversation with Majid on messenger before getting handcuffed then thrown to the floor next to my door. 'Easy, popo, I can understand instructions, you know.'

'These Pakis, don't they know by now you do the crime, you do the time?' The policeman tightened the handcuffs to deliberately hurt me.

As I struggled to get free, my mother and sister walked in screaming, 'Shak! What have you done? Let go of him! Shak, don't do this to me!' My mum got on her knees, crying her eyes out. Tara was just so shocked and kept silent. My mother grabbed me tightly by my top and nearly ripped it off with the strength she grasped it.

'Mum, I'm sorry. I didn't mean to do anything, I . . . *Aaaarrrggg!*' The officer noticed me struggling a lot to get out so he knocked me out with an elbow to the face.

Before I knew it, I was behind bars.

I've been in here too long already. I miss my mum.

Thoughts rushed out my head, giving me a headache. I was on a lower bunk of a bunk bed. Someone was on the top bunk sleeping but I didn't even want to know or see who it was. I could just smell a strong scent of cannabis coming from him. He was a black guy; I could see his arm hanging down from the bed.

I was so scared, I wanted to get out, and I didn't like the place at all. I've just been here for a short while and hate it. Before the guy from above me woke up, I thought of my mum, dad, and sister a lot, and how I've let them down. But if they only knew I shot the Big Boss because he shot Malik and it was just principle: if anyone touches my boys, I have to mess them up. It's my fault.

I thought about Naila, that she'll be getting married in two weeks. Damn, I can't do jack about it from here.

I thought about the money, if it was worth it. Thank goodness that the police didn't do me over for stealing the money. They don't even know the money existed as they did not look into what was taken. I bet the boys are loving it, spending money like it's Monopoly money, going crazy with it. I can't even sleep; the bed is so hard, the pillows are like concrete, and the blanket is so thin that I'd rather not even have one. I don't even know how long I'm in here for. Probably six years. I can't take it. I looked around this empty prison; there were just the bare necessities. I started playing with the toothpaste tube that was on the sink table.

'Yo, ma nigga, quit that out, you gonna waste it,' the cellmate spoke.

I turned around and saw that the guy looked mean, I mean a *proper* gangster. I still couldn't see his face because a small towel was covering it. I started bricking it even more as he jumped off the top bunk.

'So, you ma new cellie. What's good, ma nigga? I'm known in this joint right here as Knuckle.' He put out his fist to firms me. I noticed so many cuts on his fist. I firmed him and put down the toothpaste.

'I'm Shak,' I said with no intention of hurting Knuckle's feelings in any way whatsoever. When I say he looked mean, he looked mean.

'So, what is it you done to get locked up next to me? I don't really get on with pussyole Asian boys. They chat so much shiznit, they go on like they niggas, fuggin fake-ass Asian batty boys. So, what you in for?'

Knuckle's dreads were covering his face as he moved the towel and revealed his face. There were as many cuts on his face as there were on his fist. It frightened me. I then stopped to think, and my heart stopped for a moment. I was in the same prison; I was in the same cell, as Knuckle. No way!

'You're Knuckle? Oh, my God! I'm dreaming. You ain't really here. Hang on, you meant to be in some London prison, aren't you? What you doing here?'

I was shivering and shaking so much because Knuckle was like the roughest, meanest gangster out there.

'Yo, mai, stop trippin. I ain't Jesus or the Notorious. Just look around. This is five-star treatment compared to any London prison.' I looked around and saw a sink, toilet, and a bunk bed, but it was clean so I assumed the other cell was dirty with no essentials.

'Yo, man, I'm your biggest fan. I like chat about things you done and that with my bedrins. Sick, man. I'm in the same cell as Knuckle. This is next level.'

My fear went down a little but then came back when he smacked the wall next to me. 'This ain't no picnic, bitch. If you wanna play this game of me being a celebrity, then I'm just gonna go forward and whup your punk-ass right now. Being well known ain't shiznit when you locked up. You just part of all the rest of the convicts to the popo man, dem scum of the earth, mai.'

Knuckle sat himself down on my bunk and stated, 'You know, you gonna have to roll wiv your Indian boys, well *you* boys are Asian here, where I'm from. Asians are Chinese in America. Anyway, niggers stick with niggers, white boys with other white boys, because if you alone in this joint, you just gonna get raped, you get me? It's a keep-outta-our-way system here. Gorra have your eyes wide open, all the time.'

A hard and long week later, I was outside with some other Muslim guys at the weights bench. It was too cold, plus the weights seemed to be heavier than before, and to top it off, a gang of white supremacy skinheaded boys started trouble with us by kicking and throwing the weights at us. As soon as we fought back, the violence started. A tall white guy pushed a Muslim brother off the bench. The Muslim brother flipped as he fell to the floor.

He said, 'You gorra problem, you piece of . . .'

Smack! The white guy lamped him in his face with a weight and it basically kicked off from there. There were two black Muslims with us and the rest of us were Asian. There were fists to the face, kicks to the stomach, and hair on the head being ripped out. I picked up a few weights and started swinging them all over the place, luckily hitting a few of the guys in their faces and bodies.

I saw there were getting fewer of us due to them getting the upper hand. While I saw one of the black Muslim brothers go down, I took one hard blow to the head and dropped on the ground, and then I got the hell kicked out of me as they all ganged up around me. I was screaming inside in pain, but nothing could help me.

I opened my eyes after few more kicks to my body. I saw a guard, but he was just watching and laughing. I cried. I cried out for help, from God, from my mother, from my dad. There was none of us standing up anymore. All of us were severely injured and internally damaged. All of us were moaning as we were still getting beaten. I thought that this was it. *I'm going to die right here and no one is going to help us.* My vision also started getting blurry and dimmer.

Suddenly, I saw one of the skinheads fall to the ground, then another, then I struggled to look up, but I think I saw another gang come and begin knocking down each and every white guy. My eyes were swollen so I found it really difficult to see what was going on, but I recognised Knuckle's voice. I don't know what he was saying, but I knew he was kicking some white ass. As I knew I couldn't get beaten up anymore, I knocked out cold on the floor.

About five hours later, there were about fifteen men in the nurse's room getting bandaged up. I was thinking that I needed to thank Knuckle and his boys. I was also thinking about of how much I hated this place. I missed my mum, my sister, my boys, and Naila.

'Shak, you coming to pray, bro?' one of the brothers called.

I got up off the bed slowly and walked out the door. I looked at one of the white guys before I left the room, and he gave me such a dirty stare, a stare to say it's not over. *Well come then, white boy. I got Knuckle to back my case.* I walked out also thinking, *What if I don't have Knuckle to back my case? That means I'm going to be done for.*

I done my ablution and joined a congregation prayer which that brother started. I finished my prayer then waited to see if I had a visitor. Since I've been in prison, I've been praying all my daily prayers, which is a good thing because I only managed to pray a few before. Praying to get the hell out of here and that while I'm here it's made easy for me.

'Shakiel, you have a visitor at table seven. Please follow me. You will be handcuffed so don't try nothing, you get me, little youth?' a guard informed me.

I turned around to get handcuffed, thinking that my mum had come to see me because she had come in every day since I'd been in here. I walked in the visitor room and was shocked as I immediately noticed Naila sitting there. *She can't see me like this, in jail, all beaten up.* I sat down. The first thing I did was smell her perfume and then looked in her eyes, not knowing what to say.

'Shakiel, what happened to you? Are you hurt? What are they doing to you?' Naila shouted out as she touched my face. I didn't speak; I was in too much pain to talk *even* to her. She put her hands back and sighed. 'I know how you got here, so let's just get to the point. I'm getting married in a week, to Ali. For a week I was thinking something was going to happen to prevent it from happening, but you are gonna still be in here. I'm still gonna marry Ali whether I like it or not. I want you still, you know, even if you are a convict.'

'I . . . I . . . I waan oo . . . tooo,' I mumbled out. I put out my hand for her to hold. She put her soft hands on my hand. Naila started crying on my hand. Her warm tears ran down into my sleeves and a tear also dropped from my eye.

'I miss you so much,' I said. I coughed out 'I miss you.'

'Don't talk, let me talk, Shak. These few weeks have been the craziest time I've ever had in my life with you. I wanted it to last forever, but things ain't written how I want it or anyone wants it. I know I'm marrying Ali, but always remember this, Shakiel: I will always remember you!' Naila cried out.

'Why, why are you saying this?' I coughed. 'I won't do much for you, jus . . . jus cause you more problems . . . Plus . . . Plus, I'm in here for a long time.'

'I don't care what you could do for me. I care about you. I love you, Shakiel.' As Naila said this, she looked dead into my eyes with her watery eyes. That's when I thought that this was too serious. I could say I loved her, but it didn't come out. She was waiting for me to mumble it out, but I just couldn't say it. She waited a bit longer for me to say something but then added, 'I have to go. No one knows I've come to see you. Remember I will always remember you.' She got up, wiping her tears.

I tried saying something, but it seemed that my lips were sealed shut for some reason. Naila walked out while I watched her leave. Naila left the prison with her head down, still in tears. She bumped into someone but didn't say anything. She just walked off silently. The person was vexed and was about to swear at her but noticed that he knew her. It was Ali. He had come with his dad to see me and also to check out what a prison was like.

'What the hell is she doing here? I hope not to see Shak, because if she did just see him she's in big trouble.' Ali and his dad walked out of the prison and tried to catch up with Naila, but she had caught an oncoming bus by the time they reached the main road. Ali ran to his car with his dad, got in, and rushed to Naila's house to see what was going on.

I was still sitting at the table, feeling love building up even more for Naila. I was in another world until, 'Oi, Shakiel, get up and get in your cell before I shove this torch up where the sun don't shine.'

A guard lifted me up and dragged me to my cell. I was swearing at the guard in my mind. He had to disturb me at that delicate and precious moment. *Let me shove that torch there, see how you like it, stupid prick.*

The guard knew I was pissed off at him, so he added some more trash talk while I walked out of the visitor room. 'You think you a hot shot, don't you? You Muslims and your Ramadan fasting, starving nonsense, you ain't nothing but a bitch.'

I looked at him with fire in my eyes and wanted desperately for someone to beat the hell out of him for that. I couldn't because he was much bigger than me and I was already wounded. And he was an officer so I would get into deeper crap if I did. But if I was his size, I would have *raggo* beat the crap out of him even if I was a convict or not. I just want to get the hell out of this place. Please. Someone.

As I walked back to my cell, the guys were asking me *who the chick was.* Obviously, the other convicts don't see any women in the prison besides the nurse, who isn't that pretty, but a lot of the convicts don't mind. As long as she's a female, they would be happy. I got pushed in my cell by my guard; Knuckle was already in his bunk, rapping away. That's all he ever did in here was freestyling, rapping some old tunes, and smoking weed. I would usually join in with him when it came down to rapping the old tunes but today I didn't. I just lay in my bunk with my eyes closed, thinking. That's all I ever did in my spare time, think.

About an hour later, I remembered to thank Knuckle. 'Yo, Doggy Dogg, Knuckle, I appreciate what you done for me and my boys out there. I owe you big time.'

'Yo, neph, I only done it cause they be thinking they running the joint when we ain't around and I noticed them killing some guys so I thought let's all go join in, and when we got there, I saw it was you and my African Muslim brothers. I have to look out for ma lil cellie. You get me, ma nigga?' Knuckle replied while reaching for a firms. I firmed him as I was very grateful for what he had just done for us outside.

Knuckle came down from his bunk and sat down next to me, looking concerned. He said, 'So who's the lady in the black Power Ranger suit. Your material?' Knuckle lit up yet another spliff.

I took a deep breath and thought of how to put the situation between Naila and me in words. 'Knuckle, Doggy Dogg, it's complicated.'

CHAPTER 13

TIME WAS GOING very slow, especially when I was looking forward to doing something. Something is a big thing when you locked up. Going to eat, having a shower, or having a workout outside. Having to do chores were big things, but the thing I looked forward to most was seeing someone out there to visit me. I thought Naila would have come again to see me, but I guess she became too busy with the wedding. I guess she was just going to have to put up with Ali for the rest of her married life. I couldn't do anything about it, and that was a real big shame.

My mother visited me every day for one and a half weeks straight, and my sister's come about five times. I have no clue what's happening in the real world, as no one wants to inform me when they come. When my mum visits me, she just cries as soon as she looks into my eyes, which also makes me cry. It's hard seeing my mum like that. It's quite far coming here every day from our house; it's probably forty-five minutes if you're lucky, otherwise an hour to an hour and a half. I wish I never ever gave my mum this much trouble. It hurts so much. My sister visits me just to see if I'm not going mad in the pen. She doesn't even talk to me. She just sits there. I try to phone home if I can, but the phone is always in use when I get the time and I don't want to bother the big guys when they talking, if you get what I mean.

Every day, my cellmate and I would be making *million dollar records.* I would beatbox while he freestyles new raps. Other prisoners started loving the entertainment. I also started getting respect from the other prisoners, which was cool. They found out I popped a big timer, the Big Boss. I was scared at first—scared of the cell, the prisoners, and the guards—but as time slowly passed, I managed to make a few homeys. Well, only because I had a cellmate like the one I had to back me, and also the fact that I killed a well-known gangster out there. Quite a few guys here actually worked for the Big Boss, but they still rated me for it as he was the reason that some of them got in the pen. There were still times when I was scared, like when convicts got the electric chair and got killed off and when riots went on. Even Knuckle himself got the shivers when stuff like that was going on. Stabbings, beatings, and, to top it off, guards didn't have a clue who started it therefore everyone got caned.

A few days later and it's the wedding day of Naila and Ali. Naila's parents are going crazy trying to see if everything is sorted out for later on. Naila is nowhere to be seen, but her parents' minds are too busy on other things involving her wedding. My family—my mother and sister—are at Ali's house, relaxed and having their pictures taken with the groom. It is always the girl's side who organises and pays for the wedding, so the boy's side are always chilling. My mum told me yesterday she will visit me after the nikkah. She told me that she has to go to the wedding, otherwise she would get bombed by the family.

Today seemed to be a normal day at the prison. A Muslim brother borrowed me his Quran, so for two hours in the morning I was reading it. If ever I read the Quran, my mind would always wander off into dream world, but today while I was reading it, it felt like the words were going into my heart. As the text was in Arabic, I was trying to make out what was being said, linking words together and remembering stories I heard when I was a kid, like when Moses' name came up, soon after Pharaoh's name would come up, and I'd think about their story, or if Mary's name would came up I'd think about stories about her and Jesus.

After praying, I felt like I had spiritually gained something. It felt really special. I then went out for a morning workout with a few guys, arriving back to the cell; we all noticed the receptionist having an unknown visitor who was holding a briefcase. The visitor didn't even talk to the receptionist; he handed over a piece of paper with some handwritten words. The receptionist looked at the letter and then took the briefcase. No one knew who he was and what was in the briefcase. He didn't even give us a clue as he gave no eye contact with anyone.

Half eleven that day, all the guys were guessing what was in the case. We came to a conclusion that it was bail money and it was for Knuckle as he had the money to do anything really. But Knuckle, or any other one of us, was not called up to be questioned or leave just yet.

'Hurry up, you got two minutes to get in the car! We are extremely late!' Naila's dad yelled to everyone in the house, and there were a lot of people in the house. Busy, busy, busy everyone was. Still there were no signs of Naila's whereabouts. The family were too obsessed with how good they looked themselves than where Naila was and how she looked. If a person asked where Naila was, they would assume that she was still in her room getting ready.

Naila's mum finally went to see Naila in her room, thinking she was getting dressed, but instead Shamala was lying on her bed still in her nightwear.

'Where the—is Naila!' screamed out Naila's mum.

'She's gone,' Shamala gently answered.

'What!' howled Naila's mum. The whole house heard and rushed to the room to see what was going on.

Naila's dad went crazy, he made the whole house shake when he shouted at Shamala, and his fiery anger went out of control when he started throwing Naila's belongings on the floor. Naila's mum was crying in search for her daughter; she told the relatives to find her, phone anywhere they think she would be and go wherever she would go. She herself called Naila's mobile many times.

'There won't be a wedding today, at least not with my daughter,' Naila's dad said Ali's dad. 'No, is she there by any chance . . . I think . . . Okay . . . Is Ali all right . . . Break it down to him slowly . . . Okay, salaams.' As he put the phone down, he wiped his sweat off his forehead with his left arm. Shamala was the only still person in the house as the others were panicking while trying to find out where Naila was.

Ali's dad told Ali, who was just sitting on the sofa and having his picture taken with his relatives, about the situation. My mum heard the news but didn't think much of it; to her it was just another nervous runaway bride. Before Tara found out the news, she was excited because she would get to meet Riaz after so long, but then got really disappointed as there would be no wedding to meet him at. Ali and his dad were in vexed moods, they both started snapping at every little thing.

'She's seeing another guy, I know it,' Ali furiously stated.

Ali's dad ran up to his room, opened his wardrobe, moved some junk out of the way, and pulled out a shotgun.

'I'm gonna kill the fool who's messing wiv ma boy's girl.' At least six hundred people were waiting at the wedding hall for a wedding to happen. At least twenty people were looking for Naila. The groom and his father began looking for a guy with the bride to kill him for what he had caused.

Ali had a vague idea of who it was but wanted to be sure and see what was really going on.

Slowly, the news passed to the guests in the wedding hall and voices showered the hall room as gossip arose. More people started looking for Naila.

'I heard that Naila's already married, got a kid, and that and today she will come clean with it. That's why she isn't here,' a relative reported.

'No way. Who told you that? She's run off with a gora or a kala. She looks the type,' another relative suggested. Ali's dad was so furious that he started threatening the guests to make them tell him where Naila was. If he thought they knew, he would point his gun to their chest and make them wet themselves even though they didn't know. Obviously, Shamala was one of the people he went to and threatened first.

'Where the—is she? Tell me or I'll use this. I don't wanna use it, but I will.' Ali's dad tapped the gun on his head.

'She didn't tell me. I wish I knew,' Shamala honesty replied.

Hours went by and still there wasn't a clue where Naila was. Half the wedding guests were planning to leave after having no success in finding her. Ali's dad was getting so annoyed that he had threw a few stones at the birds in the sky in anger. Naila's mum had phoned the police; she kept having the worst thoughts where Naila could be and wanted to find her as soon as possible.

It was getting late and soon it would be dark; my mum was eating the wasted ordered food in the hall while looking out the window. My mum wasn't as worried about the situation as she should have been. She was more bothered on how I was and that she didn't go see me today.

My mum picked up her emptied plastic plate and put it in a black bag and walked to her cousins. 'I should go see Shak. He's probably waiting for me, you know,' my mum told her cousins, but they told her to stay for a little while. Tara was outside behind a bush with Riaz. 'I wanna be with you, be with you for good, you know what I mean? I mean, you got beat to death because of me. I know Shakiel had something to do with that,' Tara said as she held Riaz's hand.

He responded with, 'What you on about? That was because I owed money to someone, minor. Don't worry about that. Listen, your bro won't mind, he's a seen geeza. Trust me, me, him, and the other guys are tight. We done bare chillin' back in the day. He won't mind because he won't know for bare years, locked up and dat. We could get married and he won't even know, and when he comes out, he ain't like Scarface. He won't kill me off because I married his sister. Trust me, he's safe. He would want you to carry on wiv your life, you get me, Tara?'

'I know, but I can't keep something like marriage away from him. He's my brother. He's the only man in my house. If we got married, I wouldn't ever leave my bro out of it without knowing. My dad, my dad, I would love my dad to be there for it, but he can't because he ain't here no more. My bro is but behind bars. Basically, if I could have them, I would, for defo. I like you like I like my family and that's a lot, but I don't want to do anything still behind Shakiel's back.'

Tara walked farther into the bushes with Riaz. Tara continued, 'You know Naila? I like Naila. Recently she wanted to link me. It was strange. She asked for my number, yeah, then she said if I could have the house number and Shak's number just in case she couldn't get to me, but she never ever phoned me. Huh, is that who I think it is? Is that Naila?' Tara squinted her eyes, seeing the back of someone from a distance. It was Naila. Naila was talking to someone, but Tara could not see who it was.

'Naila!' screamed out Tara. All the people still at the hall and standing outside heard and made their way towards the scream. Riaz at once hid behind a tree so he wouldn't be seen by everyone with Tara, and Tara walked in the direction of Naila.

'At last, Naila is found. I thought we would never leave this place. She's by Tara, over there, outside.' My mum's cousin pointed outside to Tara. My mum, who had not left yet, saw Tara and then spotted Riaz who was still trying to hide behind that tree. She rushed outside with rage. The person with Naila had hid under a bush before everyone had come out and surrounded Naila, asking heaps of questions of where she was. "What's going through your mind? It's your wedding day?" "What the hell are you playing at?" Not one person besides my mum noticed Riaz trying to hide while all this was going on.

Naila's mum walked up to her crying, 'Where have you been, Naila? I've been worried sick, baby.'

'I . . . I . . .' Naila turned around to see if the other person was still there.

'Well, where the hell where you? We should have been friggin married ten hours ago,' Ali shouted.

Naila thought for a moment then the words slowly came out of her mouth. 'I was supposed to tell you earlier, Mum, Dad, err Ali. I wanted to tell you sooner but the right time never came. I don't even know how to say this, but I don't . . . I don't wanna marry you . . . but I do wanna get married today.' Naila hid her face behind a tree as though Ali was going to hit her. The people's faces were confused but Naila confessed some more as she started crying, breathing heavily, sweating, and gripping the tree for protection from the others. 'It's not you, Ali, it's me. I wanna get married today, but not to you.'

CHAPTER 14

Everyone's mouth dropped. Naila's face was bright red; her hands were so sweaty that they started slipping off the tree trunk as she stood behind it for protection from Ali and her parents.

'Well, who the hell is it you want to marry? Why didn't you tell me earlier?' demanded Naila's father.

'I tried to but I couldn't, and I wasn't completely sure as I *am* now,' Naila answered. A rustling noise came from under the bush. Everyone immediately backed up a few steps as they thought it was some kind of animal.

At the prison cell, the inmates were teasing a new convict. As he walked in, they tripped him over and started beating him to the ground. The new inmate limped to his cell saying, 'I need some water.'

'You ain't getting jack, nigga. Get outta my cell, pussyole white boy. No way am I getting this white piece of shiznit as my next cellie.' Knuckle pushed him out and then looked outside his cell towards the exit of the building. 'What a lucky sum-bitch.'

A person crawled out from under the bushes; he dusted the dirt off his clothes.

'Shakiel, what the hell you doing here?' my mum cried out. Before she walked to me, Ali's dad fired a bullet. *Boom!*

'*Aaarrrhhh!*' everyone screamed. My mum screamed, 'Shakiel, baby!'

Naila fainted in shock.

I fell to the floor, blood spraying on my mum's face. 'What the hell did you do, you stupid idiot? You shot my baby!' My mum wept tears and threw a rock at Ali's dad, which missed him completely. Naila's mum went to the aid of Naila who was unconscious against the tree.

Tara rushed to see me, crying, 'Ba, ba, no!' Tara picked up a rock full of dirt and threw it at Ali's dad violently, hitting his chest.

No one spoke; even Ali was shocked. He looked at his dad.

Ali's dad said, 'What? He ruined my wedding. I mean, *my son's* wedding, the prick, huh? Isn't he meant to be locked up? He's done a runner.'

The people behind Ali's dad had snuck away, scared of being shot at. Others managed to run away as Ali's dad walked closer to me.

I was in no state to talk. He had shot my shoulder and my mum tried stopping the blood with her *ordnu*, but large amounts of blood were pouring out. Silence. Ali's dad was expecting me to talk, but I was just taking in the pain, trying not to cry. Well, not in front of the others. The pain was too much. I couldn't take it anymore; my tears ran down my face, the pain. 'Get me a doctor,' I snivelled out.

Naila's mum grabbed her phone from her purse and dialled for the police. 'Damn, I didn't want them to get together this way,' she whispered to herself before getting through to the police.

'Hello . . . Please, someone come quick. A boy has just been shot . . . My name is Ayesha . . . Sorry, what was that . . . Oh, yes, I phoned in earlier about my missing daughter. She's found . . . Yes, I'm her mother, Naila's mother. She's here where I said the wedding would be. The boy who has been shot is also here. Someone come quick, please! He's in need of immediate attention.'

'Ma . . . Mum, don't worry, I'll be aite, Mum . . . Listen, I'm sorry.'

My mum told me, 'Shush.' She ripped her sleeve from her dress and clotted the rushing blood. Before I knew it, I had knocked out.

'It had to be done like that,' Rizwan said. 'If we showed our faces to the police, giving them that much money, surely they would've clocked on. My cousin was going to Pakistan that afternoon so I told him to do the drop off. No one knows him. That's why I sent him to do it. I know you can't hear me, but I'm sorry we didn't think of something like that sooner; you must have got shafted bare times, bro, being there for that long. Plus, the streets ain't the same without you, bro.'

Rizwan was informing me about the plan they had thought of and gone forward in doing. It was a late afternoon, three days after the shooting, and we were all at the hospital. My mum was here all day, all night; she slept in the visitors room on the chairs and she refused to go home. I was unconscious for three days straight.

Tara was here as well. She was in the dining area with my mum. Rizwan was my only visitor in my room, and he was sitting next to me. Naila and Shamala then walked in.

Rizwan stood up to give them a seat. Naila sat next to me and Shamala sat at the edge of the bed.

Naila put her hand on my forehead. 'You're crazy, Shak. You've really gone and done it now.' Naila giggled then turned to Rizwan.

'When you phoned me that morning, I had to make a life-changing decision. Shamz helped me out a lot, convincing me to leave him on the stage. Anyway, how did you get so much money to get him out?'

'I'll let Shak let you know about that but I just thought you ought to know. He couldn't stop talking about you when he was with us, about how real you were, about how you came into his life and made his dreams a reality. I'm his mate. I've never seen you in my life, but when he was telling me what you were like, I could see the love he had in his eyes for you. Remembering that, I knew I had to do something, even if it meant drastic measures, and this sounded pretty extreme when I heard about it,' Rizwan explained.

A shot of breath forced itself out my mouth. I coughed.

'Maaa . . .'

'It's me, Shakiel, Naila. Can you hear me? Call his mum or a nurse. I seen his mum downstairs. Shakiel, can you hear me?' Naila pointed to the door for Rizwan to call someone to help. Naila tried communicating with me but I was struggling to hear, speak, or move.

The door slammed open. My mum walked in and said, 'Shakiel, you all right? Shakiel, can you hear me?'

'Mum, Mum, is that you?' I blinked and coughed again. 'Ma, I told you not to worry. I'm aite. This is nothing.'

Naila, Rizwan, and Shamala giggled in joy, but my mum let out tears and cried, 'I thought I'd lose you too. Can't live through that again, Shakiel.' My mother reached out and touched my head to see if my temperature was fine. She then sat on the bed next to Naila and smiled.

'Shakiel, I got good news for you.' Naila looked down as she got bashful. It was the first time she was talking to me in front of my mum and me being awake.

'We had to come to a final decision, my parents and . . . errm . . . your mum, a decision that, if you agree to, both of us should get engaged in two weeks. The doctors say you will recover in a few more days. Everyone knows about us, Shak.' Naila giggled out cheerfully.

As soon as I heard 'engaged,' I was ready to agree to it. I said, 'But what about Ali? What about . . .' I looked at my shoulder.

'Ali is screwing, not over losing me but his dad. He's locked up for shooting you, but he'll be out soon because you are okay. Ali told me that I was the worst thing in his life anyway. Forget him and about your shoulder—that's going to heal. Even if it doesn't, I don't care. You know why? Because I love you. I do, Shakiel.'

My mum and I looked at Naila shockingly, whereas Rizwan and Shamala already knew her true feelings and they both sighed.

I couldn't believe my mum knew. I had kept it away from her for so long. Butterflies fluttered in my stomach as I replied, 'Mum, if it's all right with you, then, yeah, can I get . . . err . . . engaged to . . . err . . . her in two weeks?'

My mum, still tearful, answered, 'Yes, make me proud, son. Your dad would've liked her too.' My mum wiped her tears and faced Naila. 'I know you haven't started on the right foot in this relationship, but no one on earth is perfect and no one can control who their heart goes for.' My mum smiled at me then sat on the bed. I felt I accomplished something huge without doing anything. I mean, after being shot, I was so happy. I was even more happy because my mum was happy.

Unexpectedly, Tara walked in, surprised to see me awake. She was about to say something but paused and closed her mouth and just gave me a smile. I assumed Tara knew what the situation was, so I said, 'You aite, Tara. You couldn't get rid of me that quick, so you gonna be a sister-in-law. What d'you think about that?'

'Mubarak Shak, it's a shame I can't spend time with you guys when you get together.' Tara also assumed that I knew something else.

I confusingly questioned, 'What d'you mean? We ain't going anywhere, are we?'

Tara answered while walking behind our mum, 'Haven't they told you that I'm getting married the same day as you next year? Mum goes she didn't want any secrets from us anymore behind her back like. It's . . . it's Riaz.'

Everyone looked at me to see my reactions. I crushed my fist. I wish Riaz's head was between my fingers.

'This ain't going down like this, trust me. I'm gonna kill that prick right now.' I got off the bed but my mum and Rizwan stopped me and lay me back down.

'You ain't going now where, not in this state, you ain't. Listen, I've agreed to it. Riaz's parents have too. You ain't gonna do nothing, you understood?' My mum pulled the covers over me again.

'Mum, she's too young. He's young and dumb too. Trust me, Mum, okay? You wanna get them set up, let it be in a few years or at least two. You got to understand I got mates that have got married at their age and they struggling day by day. Look, two years, that's all,' I argued.

'Shakiel, you lucky to be alive right now. Every day when you were in prison, I was scared to death worrying if you were gonna last a day longer. I was praying day and night that nothing bad would happen to you. I was praying that one day I would see you out again, but when I did, I didn't expect it to be like this. I been getting grief from all our family and friends that I'm a bad mum: son going in jail for killing someone, daughter for being stupid for playing you like this, he he.

'Shakiel, she's just messing around with you. She won't be getting married for a while. Each one of you are special to me and deserve the best so I decided to do hers a year after yours. Your *sagai* is in two weeks though,' my mum laughed.

'Mum, don't do that to me. I nearly had a heart attack. I would've gone and killed someone and they would've chucked me back into prison. Hold on, did you say Riaz? Are you gonna take that mum?' I giggled, knowing Tara would get shouted at.

'She got what she deserved; I gave her a few slaps with it.' My mum looked at Tara, as Tara rubbed her cheeks.

'We just click, that's all. We really good friends too. Is that not allowed?' Tara gently smacked my bed. As if.

'Honestly, you know, I never thought I'd see you guys again. Before I got knocked out, I thought of my dad, dad, thought of you mum, Tara, I even thought of you . . . err . . . Naila, thought that I'd never see you again. I cried inside and out. I was worried that he would have shot you guys and I couldn't have done anything about it. I'll thank God every day of my life now. Life's too precious. We have to look after it. He he! I got to look after an extra life now.'

I sat up and reached for Naila's hand. 'God's given me a life really special here.' I looked into Naila's eyes then saw my mum looking at me so I added quickly, 'I mean, he's blessed me with Naila and can't forget my main girl, you mum. You know you my one and only.'

A week later, I was out of the hospital and on my feet, fresh air in my lungs and a better-sounding heartbeat. I couldn't believe what had happened in this month alone. Naila coming into my life, the big robbery, the prison sentence, getting shot, and I'll be getting engaged in a few days.

Rizwan came to me as soon as I left the hospital concerning the cash. Rizwan and I split the money between four of us. We all got the same amount we intentionally were going to get anyway; Malik's funeral fees, the bail money and paying Rizwan's cousin to do the job came up to £580,000, so we all got £600,000 each. The £20,000 that was remaining we thought we'd left for a rainy day. Rizwan and I had a special present waiting for us whenever we want to have it. A present holding £2.5 million each.

The first thing I did was take my driving test, it was difficult but by God's will, I passed it. I was so chuffed and my mum looked even more pleased as it was one of the first achievements I got through genuine effort. Secondly, I dropped five grand on my mum's lap. I saw a tear come out but only because she knew I had done something bad to get it. I gave my sister one grand. Giving that much money to a girl her age, I knew she would go wild and she did. So wild that she pushed me out the way to get her jacket, rang her friends, and made her way to High Street. I knew I should have just given her one hundred pounds; she would've done the same thing. Even fifty quid.

I was just glad I got my driving licence sorted. That was a big relief to me. I began applying for jobs and was getting positive feedback on delivery vacancies for some reason. Which was something, I know. I knew I had to do something legitimate to make things better. I know I am not the best person in the world but God didn't want me in prison, it's like He is giving me another chance. I don't want to blow it this time. I'm going to change. Step by step. I wanted to do something for my mum, bigger than just giving her money. When I gave her the money, it didn't even feel right. Money is temporary; it will come and it will go. What can I give her that will always remain with her? I thought for a bit then I walked into the kitchen from my bedroom, folding my money and putting it in my back pocket.

As soon as I saw her face, words flowed out my mouth like a river. 'Mum, I want you to know I love you. I always have and always will. I'm sorry for being so bad. I'm sorry for Tara's mistakes. It's all my fault. I want you to know I'm to blame for every little thing that went wrong in our lives. I realised money ain't the answer for my mistakes. I need to apologise for everything I've done, everything I'm going to do—I'm still gonna do dumb stuff, stupid things, that's only because I'm a stupid bad boy. I'm sorry, Mum, I just want you to know I love you forever and I'm gonna try make things right by being a good son from now on and a better brother to Tara. Forgive me, Mum, and thank you for everything. You are truly the best.'

I didn't let her say anything; I just walked out from the kitchen, seeing yet another tear coming from my mum's eyes.

I walked back into my room thinking that even that wasn't enough to repay my mother for all she'd done for us.

I was really excited about the engagement. Every few hours, I rang Naila to see what she was doing. Usually she had just got up from the TV room to go wash in the kitchen or from doing her hair to her cleaning around the house. Basically, whatever she done in the day, I knew about it but she didn't mind.

Before I knew it, the week flew by. Preparation for the engagement party was done and I was already in-between Majid and my pretty, beautiful fiancée, Naila. As we were taking pictures, I overheard Zara from behind us saying, 'I knew about this time back but just kept my mouth shut.'

Naila and I looked at each other, remembering the time Zara caught us eating together, and we both giggled.

We ended up inviting Uncle Rafik and his family due to him being blood relatives to Naila's side of the family. Ali and his family were invited but chose not to come; they had their reasons.

Tara was surprisingly good today, she didn't even glimpse at Riaz. I didn't let my mum do any work, but she didn't listen to me. She insisted to make my engagement day the best day of my life so far, and she did. She did by just being there.

Wherever my dad was, I mean, this is how I see it: the dead are still in their graves until judgement day, but somehow they still know what's going on. They are still watching us somehow, and my dad was watching me become a man from being his little son.

Naila also seemed to be emotional. I noticed this due to her giving fake smiles in pictures. I remembered her telling me one day that her grandmother had passed away and how special it would've been if she could see her happy.

'Don't worry, I'm here, baby.' I held her hand and glanced in her eyes. I saw her eyes sparkle like diamonds. She is so beautiful. She was worth it.

Jazakallah.

GLOSSARY

Asr—Islamic afternoon prayer

Fajr—Islamic morning prayer

Masjid—Islamic praying place

Nafs—Inner desires

Choon—Tell me/us

Buudie—Old lady

Subhanallah—Glory be to God

Jazakallah—All thanks to God

Inshallah—If God wills

Kabarstaan—Graveyard

Jamaat—Congregation prayer

Nikkah—Wedding

AFTERWORD

The characters in this novel are not depicting any people in real life. Most of the characters are Muslim and living the thug life, but in reality there is no such thing as a Muslim gangster. You can either be a Muslim or a gangster; you cannot be both. You are contradicting your principles if you think in that way.

I said cool, fire me from this hundred thousand dollar movie because I ain't gonna play no gangbanger that's a Muslim. There ain't no such thing. I refuse to play parts that don't exist.

(Tupac Shakur)